Denim Diaries 6:

Lying to Live

Denim Diaries 6:

Lying to Live

Darrien Lee

URBAN Renaissance

www.urbanbooks.net

Urban Books, LLC
78 East Industry Court
Deer Park, NY 11729

Denim Diaries 6: Lying to Live Copyright © 2012 Darrien Lee

ISBN 13: 978-1-60162-363-8
ISBN 10: 1-60162-363-1

First Trade Paperback Printing September 2012
Printed in the United States of America

10 9 8 7 6 5 4 3 2 1

This is a work of fiction. Any references or similarities to actual events, real people, living or dead, or to real locales are intended to give the novel a sense of reality. Any similarity in other names, characters, places, and incidents is entirely coincidental.

Distributed by Kensington Publishing Corp.
Submit Wholesale Orders to:
Kensington Publishing Corp.
C/O Penguin Group (USA) Inc.
Attention: Order Processing
405 Murray Hill Parkway
East Rutherford, NJ 07073-2316
Phone: 1-800-526-0275
Fax: 1-800-227-9604

Denim Diaries 6:

Lying to Live

by
Darrien Lee

Prologue

The smell of the gunpowder filled the store, and the sound of the shotgun blast had Julius's ears ringing. As he stood hidden behind the potato chip stand, he could hear the cashier moaning in agony as the robber ravaged the cash register. Surely, someone had heard the gunshot and had called police, but oddly, he didn't hear any sirens. A few seconds later Julius realized that the robber was walking down the aisle next to where he was hiding to get a case of beer. He came so close to him that if he had taken one more step, Julius would've been discovered. Julius held his breath as he saw a familiar face from the neighborhood in the reflection of the freezer doors. He couldn't move or breathe as he listened to his heartbeat get louder and louder. A second later he watched the man tuck the case of beer under his arm and exit out the front door. Only then did Julius allow himself to breathe. He knew he had to do something, so with trembling hands he opened his cell phone and dialed 911.

"Nine-one-one. What is your emergency?" the operator said through the telephone.

When Julius tried to speak, no words would come out, so he swallowed the lump in his throat and tried again.

"There's been a shooting."

"Speak up, sir. I can barely hear you," the operator replied.

"Benny's Market on the corner of Elk and Littleton has been robbed. I came in to buy a soda, and some guy came in and robbed and shot Remy."

"Who is Remy, sir?" the operator asked.

"He's the clerk at the store," he answered.

Julius could hear the operator typing on her keyboard as she continued to ask him questions.

"Police and medics are on the way. Is the robber still in the store?"

"I heard him leave out the front door," he whispered.

"What is your name?" the operator asked.

"Julius. Julius Graham."

"How old are you?"

"I'm fourteen," he answered nervously.

"Are you injured, Julius?" she asked.

"No, ma'am, but I think Remy's dead."

"It's going to be okay, Julius. You're doing great," the operator replied when she detected tension in the young man's voice. "Stay on the line until I let you know you can hang up."

Julius could hear the operator relaying his position and other information to police officers.

"Julius, the police would like a description of your clothing."

He looked down at himself and said, "I have on some jeans and a green shirt with yellow stripes."

"You're doing great, Julius. Police should be arriving any second."

"I hear sirens," he replied. "Is it okay for me to get up?"

"No, Julius. Let them come to you. I've given them your position. Don't move."

"Yes, ma'am."

Seconds later Julius heard police enter the store.

"Police!"

"They're here," Julius told the operator.

"They know where you are," she stated. "Stay calm."

A second later two police officers approached him from both sides with guns drawn.

"Julius?" one of the officers asked.

"Yes, sir."

"We got him!" the officer yelled into his radio. He then took the cell phone out of Julius's hand and said, "Dispatch, we have the kid."

Chapter One

Everything seemed to be moving in fast-forward. There were police everywhere, and a crowd had gathered outside the store. The police patted Julius down before escorting him into the store office, while paramedics checked on the clerk . Seconds later two Arrington homicide detectives entered the office to get a statement from Julius while his memory was fresh. A third detective prepared to check the store's surveillance cameras to see if the crime had been captured on videotape. After getting Julius's complete name and address, the two detectives introduced themselves to the teenager.

"Julius, I'm Detective Daniels, and this is Detective Young. We want to take you downtown so we can talk to you in private about what happened here tonight."

"I need to call my parents," Julius announced nervously.

"Don't worry. We sent a police officer to your house to talk to your parents. They're going to meet us at the precinct," Detective Daniels answered.

Julius looked up at the detectives with tears in his eyes and said, "I'd really like to speak to my dad. Please?"

"Okay," Detective Young replied as he gave Julius his cell phone back so he could call his dad.

Julius dialed his father's number and waited for him to answer. Once he heard his father's voice, he felt relieved.

"Dad, are you on your way to get me?"

"Of course I am. Are you hurt?" his father asked.

"No, sir, I'm fine. Just a little shaken up."

"I know you're scared, son, but be strong, and don't say a word to the detectives until I get there. By law, they can't question you without me or your mother being there."

"But, Dad—"

"No buts, Julius," his father said, interrupting him. "You know how things are in our neighborhood. If the person who did this finds out you're talking to the cops, I would hate to think what could happen. Understand?"

"Yes, sir."

"Good! So if they start questioning you, just tell them you want to wait until your parents arrive. Okay?"

"Yes, sir."

Julius hung up his cell phone just as a police officer walked into the office. He whispered something to the detectives before walking back out into the store.

Detective Daniels sighed and then put his hand on Julius's shoulder. "Julius, I'm sorry to tell you this, but the cashier didn't make it. Now you see how important it is to tell us everything that happened here tonight."

Julius lowered his head and said, "I want to help, but this is a tough neighborhood. If people see me coming out of here, they're going to think I'm a snitch. I'll be dead in twenty-four hours."

"Don't worry, young man," Detective Daniels stated. "No one knows you're here, and to be safe, we're going to take you out the back door and shield you as much as possible."

"Promise?" Julius asked.

"Promise," Detective Daniels replied.

"Julius, if you can identify the shooter, you have to tell us."

Julius hesitated and then answered, "I want to wait until my parents are with me."

The detective motioned for Julius to stand up and said, "You have to trust us so we can catch the guy who did."

The choice was no longer in Julius's hands, because he was a minor, but he would have to become a man sooner than he had ever expected. In the meantime he would do his best not to get himself and his family killed. The person he saw in the reflection of the freezer was not a person anyone wanted to cross, and he hoped he never had to.

At the police station he was greeted by his frantic parents. His mother examined him to make sure he wasn't injured. His father spoke with the detectives before accompanying his son into the chilly interrogation room, while his mother waited in a conference room with a hot cup of coffee. The two detectives entered the interrogation room with coffee for Julius's father and hot cocoa for Julius.

"Mr. Graham, we appreciate you allowing us to interview your son. The sooner we can put the person responsible for this homicide behind bars, the better it will be for the victim's family and everyone in your neighborhood," Detective Daniels said.

Mr. Graham leaned forward and said, "Detective Daniels, I'm going to be straight up with you. We didn't come down here to put our son's life at risk. I only came down here to get my boy. You're going to have to catch the killer another way."

Detective Daniels looked at Mr. Graham and said, "Sir, I don't think you understand. There's a killer on the streets of your neighborhood, and your son is the only person who can help us catch him."

"Detective, there are a lot of killers on the streets of my neighborhood. My son is not saying a word," Mr. Graham announced as he stood. "We're walking out of here . . . now."

"Please, Mr. Graham. We really need your cooperation," the detective stressed.

Julius's father reached for the doorknob and yelled, "I said we're leaving! And if you continue to harass my son, I'm going to hire an attorney to protect my son's rights."

"Mr. Graham, Julius was in the store at the time of the murder, and if we can't get you to cooperate, the evidence could steer our investigation in a different direction."

Julius's father turned to face the detective and asked, "Are you threatening me?"

"All I'm saying is that I won't be able to stop the DA if he decides to look at Julius as a possible accomplice instead of a witness for the prosecution. Until we have a chance to interview him properly, we have no choice but to consider an alternate theory."

Mr. Graham walked over to Detective Daniels and pointed his finger in his face. "You have lost your damn mind if you think I'm going to stand here and let you try to accuse my son of this bullshit. Do what you have to do, and I'll do what I have to do to protect my child. This conversation is over and we're out of here, and if you have anything else to say to my son, you'll have to go through me and my attorney, and believe me, it'll be harder to get past me than my attorney."

The detectives had no choice but to allow Julius to leave with his parents. The detectives watched as the Graham family walked out of the office and onto the elevator.

"He'll be back," Detective Daniels stated.

Detective Young turned to his partner and replied, "I think you're wrong, partner."

They returned to their office and sat down at their desks and started going over the case.

"Did you see the look in that kid's eyes?" Detective Daniels asked. "He wants to talk, but his dad won't let him."

"I can't say I blame him," Detective Young replied as he typed some information into his computer. "It's a tough area over there now. I can remember when it was one of the better neighborhoods in the area. It was full of hard-working, middle-class, and retired families. Now look at it. Crime has done a number on it for sure. The people that could move out did, and those who can't feel trapped. That area has caught at least three homicides this year, and none of them have been solved. Somebody over there will eventually have to step up, and Julius might be our only hope."

"Don't hold your breath," Detective Daniels answered. "His father's not a pushover, and he's not having it."

The ride back to the Graham house was relatively quiet. At least it was until Julius's mother turned to him and said, "Sweetheart, are you okay?"

"No, Mom, I'm not okay. I watched a friend of mine die tonight."

His father looked at him through the rearview mirror and said, "Boy, watch your tone with your mother."

"I'm sorry, Dad."

"Don't apologize to me," his father answered in a disappointed tone of voice. "Apologize to your mother."

"I'm sorry, Mom."

She reached over the seat and took her son's hand in hers and gave it a squeeze. "Apology accepted, son. It's been a scary night for all of us. Once we get home and get some sleep, we can talk about this in the morning. The main thing is that you're safe. You could've been killed."

Mr. Graham looked up in the mirror again and said, "Your mother is right, and the only way you're going to stay safe is to keep your mouth shut. Just remember, whoever did this is still on the streets, and they won't think twice about killing you if they think you know something. Do you understand where I'm coming from?"

"Yes, sir."

"Good. Now, there's no reason to talk about this anymore. We need to treat this like it never happened."

Julius's mom looked over at her husband in shock and said, "Paul Michael Graham! Are you listening to yourself? Is this what you want to teach your son? A man is dead!"

He pulled into their driveway and put the car in park. He turned to his wife and said, "I know a man is dead, and I'm sorry about that, but it's my job to keep my family alive, and if I have to go against everything I believe in to do it, so be it. I will not lose my family to the streets."

She opened the car door and stepped out of the car, slamming the door behind her.

"Come on, Alecia," Mr. Graham pleaded with his wife as he climbed out of the car. "I need you to support me on this."

When she turned to respond to him, shots rang out and all three of them fell to the ground.

Chapter Two

Denim tossed and turned in bed. She couldn't understand why she was having such a hard time falling asleep. She didn't have anything in particular on her mind. She had gotten a twenty-six on her ACT test, and her relationship with Dré had never been better. Things at work were good, so that couldn't be the source of her stress. She felt anxious, nervous, and she needed someone to talk to in order to calm her nerves, and who best to calm her nerves but the love of life? It was nearly midnight, but time didn't matter when they really needed to hear each other's voice. She picked up her cell phone and sent him a text message to see if he was awake. Within seconds her cell phone vibrated, alerting her to a phone call.

"Hello, babe," he greeted her in a sleepy tone of voice.

"I'm sorry. Did I wake you?" she asked.

"Yeah, but it's cool," he reassured her. "What's up?"

"I can't sleep," she replied with a slight purr.

He yawned before answering. "What's got you so restless?"

She rolled over onto her back and said, "I don't know. For some reason I feel like it's the calm before the storm or something. It's hard to explain."

Being a typical teenage boy, he asked, "Why don't I come over and give you my special sleeping pill? It's guaranteed to put you right to sleep."

Denim giggled and said, "You might have a special sleeping pill, but my daddy has a special shotgun with your name written all over it."

Dré laughed and said, "True that. Your dad doesn't play, but you're worth the risk."

"That's sweet, Dré. You always know how to stop me from stressing. Thanks for making me smile."

"You're welcome. Now do you feel better?" he asked with concern.

"Yes, but I would feel even better if I could get one of your hugs."

"Don't tempt me, Cocoa Princess. You know it'll only take me about ten minutes to get to your house."

Denim closed her eyes and envisioned herself in his arms. It was where she felt calm and secure.

"I love you, Dré," she whispered.

"I love you too," he whispered seductively back to her. "Listen, try to get some sleep. Just think happy thoughts, and you'll be asleep in no time. If it still doesn't work, call me back, and we'll talk until you feel sleepy."

"Thanks, babe. I'm going to take your advice and think happy thoughts, but as soon as I see you in the morning, I need a big hug and a kiss with those luscious lips."

"That's a date. Sweet dreams," he said before hanging up the telephone.

Denim sat her cell phone on her nightstand and stared out the window at the full moon. It was a breezy night, and the branches from the tree outside her window gently scratched against her windowpane. Feeling a little more relaxed, she turned on her satellite radio and put it on an easy listening station. Within twenty minutes she was sound asleep.

***

Across town, sleep wasn't going to come easily for the Graham family anytime soon. By the time they felt safe enough to get off the ground, they quickly made their way inside the house. Only then did they realize the shots had been fired one street over from theirs. It had sounded so close, and for a moment they'd thought they were the target.

"That was close," Mrs. Graham stated, nearly hyperventilating as she leaned against the wall in the family room.

"Yeah, too close," Mr. Graham replied as he cautiously peeped out through the curtains.

"Where's Zakia?" Julius asked frantically. Zakia was his eight-year-old sister, who he adored.

"She's okay," his mother revealed. "She's next door with Mr. and Mrs. Spence. They said they would keep her for the night."

Mrs. Spence was a sixty-something-year-old retired nurse, and her husband, also retired, used to work in security.

"Mom, you didn't tell them what happened, did you?" Julius asked.

Mrs. Graham looked over at her husband for assistance. He was checking the windows and doors to make sure they were locked and secured.

"Julius, the Spences know, but you don't have to worry about them telling anyone anything. They're the one family in this neighborhood we can trust," he said while peeping out the window. "Those shots sound like they were coming from down the block. I have got to get us out of this neighborhood before someone gets killed."

"Dad, I don't feel right with Zakia not being here."

He looked over at his son and said, "Your sister is fine. Besides, it's late, and I know she's asleep by now."

Mr. Graham could see the worry on Julius's face, and it bothered him.

"Alecia, maybe you and the kids should stay with your mother until I can find another place to live."

Mrs. Graham stared at her husband in disbelief. She understood he wanted to keep the family safe, but she couldn't leave her job, nor did she think it was wise to take Julius out of his school. "You're not going to split up our family."

"I will if it'll keep you guys safe," he responded as he folded his arms defensively.

Mrs. Graham hugged Julius before wishing him a good night. Once he was out of the room, she turned to Mr. Graham and said, "You're not splitting this family up, so you can forget that. Staying with my parents will add over an hour to my commute to work each day, and I can't afford to be late, putting my job at risk. We're barely hanging on now."

"Don't you think I know that?" he yelled at her. "How do you think it makes me feel not to be able to provide for this family and keep you safe? Cut me some slack, Alecia. Damn! I'm doing the best I can!"

Emotions were running even higher in the Graham family, and it didn't take much to set either one of them off. Mr. Graham loved his family, and the last thing he wanted was for them to be without necessities. His family meant everything to him, and protecting them and providing for them were his main priorities.

Mrs. Graham walked over to her husband and wrapped her arms around his waist to comfort him.

"I'm sorry, Paul. I didn't mean to sound unappreciative," she said in a soft, soothing voice as she massaged his back. "Baby, I know you're doing the best you can right now. So many people are out of work, and this is going to be an uphill battle for us, but we'll get through it. We always do. Our chances of finding somewhere safe to live with our budget and one income are going to be slim to none right now."

"We'll work it out," he replied as he kissed her on the lips. "I'm sorry I yelled at you. I know you're just as stressed about this situation as I am. We're family, and we're going to get through this as a family. I never in my wildest dreams would've thought in only ten years this neighborhood would go to hell like this. Tomorrow we'll sit down and work this out. Our children will not grow up in this environment. Agreed?"

"Agreed," Mrs. Graham answered as she led him toward the stairs. "What about Julius? How are we going to handle the police? We can't afford an attorney right now."

"You let me worry that. Those detectives are not going to pressure him into a corner. It's late, and you and Julius need to go to bed."

"Aren't you coming to bed too?" she asked while caressing his hand.

"I will shortly. I need time to decompress from everything that's happened tonight, and I want to make sure things quiet down before I turn in. There's still a lot of sirens in the area and people on the streets."

She leaned in and gave him a tender kiss on the lips. "Good night, sweetheart. Don't stay up too long, and look in on Julius before you come to bed."

"I will. Good night."

"Good night."

Mr. Graham ended up watching TV until those boring infomercials came on.. He fell asleep on the sofa with his 9mm by his side. He had armed himself just in case there was trouble, and he would die before he let anyone hurt his family.

Over the next few nights Julius had trouble sleeping. He spent countless hours replaying the robbery over in his mind. No matter how hard he tried to forget, he could still smell the smoke from the gun, and his ears were still ringing from the loud blast. Each night he tried different methods to try to go to sleep. One night he worked out with his weights before bed. He figured if he wore himself out, he would crash, but it didn't work. The next night he took a hot bath and listened to tranquil music, but that didn't work, either.

He was stressing not only over the robbery but over his parents too. He'd heard them arguing a few nights ago, and he actually agreed with both of them. The best solution to their problem was his father finding another manager's job so they could get out of this crime-infested neighborhood, but unfortunately, it might take a while, since the recession had hit. In the meantime he decided he would do what he could to find a job to help out around the house. A lot of companies were willing to hire teens over adults because they were cheaper labor and most times they didn't have to provide benefits for them. The recession was making life hard on many people, which in turn made crime rise even higher. His mind was made up. A job would ease some of the financial strain his family was under, and no time was better than now for him to start searching. Since he couldn't sleep, anyway, Julius turned on his laptop and started searching the classifieds. The sooner he looked for a job, the sooner he'd find one.

"Julius, wake up," Mrs. Graham whispered to her son, who had fallen asleep with his laptop.

Startled, he asked, "What's wrong?"

She smiled and said, "You fell asleep with your laptop. This is not the way to get some rest.

Were you up most of the night on Facebook again?"

He sat the laptop on his nightstand and said, "No, ma'am, I was looking for a job."

Mrs. Graham walked over to his window and opened the curtains to let the sun in.

"Sweetheart, your schoolwork is much more important to us than you working. Don't you want to go to college?"

He crawled out of bed and said, "But, Mom, I want to help. Since Dad can't find a job right now, maybe I can."

She hugged her son and said, "It's sweet of you to want to help, but we'll be okay."

Julius stepped out of his mother's embrace and asked, "When? We're stuck here until we can afford to move. If anyone finds out that I was in the store during the robbery, we're dead."

Mrs. Graham could see the anxiety in her son's eyes, and she could feel his struggle between doing what was right and protecting the family. She sat down on the side of his bed and asked, "What do you want to do, son?"

"I want to feel safe, and I want us to live somewhere safe."

She hugged his neck and said, "That's what we want too, son, but it might take a little longer than we planned. You just concentrate on your grades, and your father and I will work out everything else."

"But, Mom . . ."

Mrs. Graham stood and said, "Julius, please. We got this. Now, get dressed so you can eat breakfast before you leave for school."

"Yes, ma'am," he answered as he made his way toward the bathroom, but before he could get there, Zakia ran into the room and jumped on his back.

"Zakia, get off your brother's back," Mrs. Graham instructed her.

Julius twirled his sister around and said, "She's okay, Mom."

Mrs. Graham grabbed his dirty clothes hamper and walked out into the hallway and said, "You two don't have long to play, or you're going to miss the bus."

"We'll be ready, Mom," Julius answered as he playfully tossed his sister on the bed and tickled her.

Zakia giggled and begged for him to stop. When he did, he looked into her beautiful brown eyes and said, "You know you're my favorite sister, right?"

"Silly head, I'm your only sister."

"That's right," he answered as he grabbed her foot and started tickling it.

"You two need to stop playing and get ready for school," Mrs. Graham said as she passed by the room with Zakia's dirty laundry.

"Okay, Mom," Julius replied. "Zakia, get dressed so I can walk you to the bus stop."

She kissed him on the cheek and said, "Okay!"

An hour later Julius slowly made his way down the street with Zakia right by his side. She was talking a mile a minute about the latest episode of the TV show *Glee*. Once they reached the bus stop, her bus came almost immediately. Before she boarded it, he reminded her to call him if she needed anything. She nodded and gave him a kiss on the cheek before climbing on the bus. After Zakia's bus pulled away from the curb and while waiting for his own bus, he put his earplugs in his ears and tucked his iPod in his pocket. The last thing he wanted was to get jacked for his iPod, and there were plenty of bullies in the neighborhood who took advantage of kids like him all the time. Luckily for him, he looked older than fourteen, so he didn't become a target as much as other kids did. At the bus stop he normally didn't socialize with the other kids unless his best friend Domingo was there. Domingo rode the bus only when he didn't ride to school with his cousin. Most of the other kids were still too sleepy to socialize, and there were a few who kept themselves occupied with texting, talking on their cell phones, or listening to music. There were a few who actually studied at the bus stop, but it was mostly girls. Julian continued to listen to the sounds of Drake, Trey Songz, and Lil Wayne until Domingo walked over and shook his hand.

"What's up, Julius?"

Julius turned off his iPod and said, "Nothing much. Still trying to wake up. I haven't been sleeping much lately."

"I'm right there with you. Did you hear about that store clerk getting blasted a few nights ago?"

Julius lowered his eyes and said, "Yeah, I heard about it. Remy was cool. I hate that somebody took him out like that."

Domingo moved closer to Julius and said, "Word on the street is that Viper did it."

There it was. Julius didn't want to think about it or even admit it to himself, but now it was a reality for sure. Viper was approximately twenty years old and had long blond dreadlocks. He had a long criminal history and spent most of his juvenile life in and out of jail. Now he had graduated to murder, and there was nothing he wouldn't do to stay out of jail, including killing Julius.

"Who told you Viper did it?" Julius asked curiously as he looked around to make sure no one could hear their conversation.

"I said it was word on the street," Domingo replied. "There's also a rumor that the police are going door to door, looking for somebody who might've seen something or been in the store at the time."

Julius's heart started pounding in his chest. He knew he couldn't trust the police.

"What kind of witness?" Julius asked.

"I don't know, but if Viper finds out there's somebody out there who could get him locked, there's going to be another murder."

Concerned for his safety even more, Julius asked, "Who told you all this information?"

"Bro, I told you it's just talk in the streets. If you hung out on the basketball court more often, you would know what was going on."

Julius shook his head and said, "I know, but my time is going to be even shorter now that I have a tutor to help me with my grades, especially in algebra."

Domingo playfully pushed him and said, "I didn't know you were failing algebra."

Julius pushed him back and said, "I'm not failing, but I have a C, and I want to bring it up."

"That's cool," Domingo replied as the bus pulled up.

As the teens waited their turn to get on the bus, Domingo turned to Julius and said, "I'd better see you on the basketball court on the days you're not getting tutored, because I know you and I both know you have game."

"I'll be there," Julius answered as they found a seat together on the bus. On the ride to school Julius's heart rate accelerated again as he thought about Viper. If what Domingo had said was true, he was going to have to watch his back very carefully and make sure Viper never found out he was the witness the police were trying to flush out.

Chapter Three

Denim sat in the library with Dré as she waited for her new client at the physical therapy clinic where she assisted as a technician. Both were studying for upcoming exams, and this also gave them a little time to spend together before they had to go their separate ways. Denim was off work today, but Dré had to meet the basketball team in the weight room for weight training. Just then her cell phone vibrated. She read the message and then blushed. She looked up at Dré and whispered, "You are going to have to stop sending me these nasty messages. What if my parents accidentally see them?"

"I can't help myself," he admitted to her. "It's your responsibility to delete them out of your phone. I love you, so you're going to get messages like that from me. I'm joking around most of the time, but you know how I feel about you."

Tears formed in Denim's eyes as she got up, walked around the table, and hugged his neck. She gave him a tender kiss on the lips and said, "I love you too, Dré."

"I'd better go," he said, then stood and gave her a warm hug and a kiss on the lips. The young couple looked around to make sure the librarian hadn't seen them. He started putting his books in his book bag just as Julius walked up.

"Are you Denim Mitchell?" he asked nervously.

Denim smiled and held out her hand and said, "I am. And you must be Julius. It's nice to meet you."

Julius placed his book bag on the chair and said, "It's nice to meet you too."

Denim pointed at Dré and said, "Julius, this is my boyfriend, André Patterson. Dré, this is Julius Graham, my new client."

Julius shook Dré's hand and said, "I know who you are. You've been on the cover of every newspaper in the state. You have some mad skills on the court."

"Thanks, Julius," Dré humbly replied. "You're a freshman, right?"

"Yeah."

"You're tall for your age, and you have big hands. Do you play ball?" Dré asked.

"A little bit. Mostly around the neighborhood with friends."

"You should think about going out for the team."

Flattered that Dré had made such a suggestion, Julius answered, "I'll think about it."

"Good," Dré answered before turning to give Denim one last kiss. "I hate to leave you two, but I have to go work out. I'll see you later."

Denim blushed and said, "Have a good workout."

"I will," he replied. "Julius, you're in good hands, and take care of my girl for me while I'm gone."

Julius gave Dré one last handshake before he walked away and said, "I'll try."

Denim turned to Julius and asked, "Are you ready to get started?"

"I guess," he answered as he sat down and opened up his book.

"Okay, we have an hour, so show me what you're studying in your class and what you have the most problem with, and we'll go from there."

He smiled and began to show Denim his lesson plan. An hour later she felt like she had made a lot of progress with Julius.

"You did great, Julius. You'll have that A in no time."

Julius gathered his books and said, "I hope so. I appreciate you helping me."

"It's my pleasure," she answered as she checked her cell phone for messages.

"Thanks again," he said as he handed her the money to pay for his session.

She tucked the money into her pocket and said, "You don't have to pay me daily if you don't want to. You can do whatever is easiest for you and your parents."

"I know, but I'd rather do it this way, if it's okay with you."

"Cool," she answered they walked toward the exit together. Once outside Julius noticed his father parked outside the school with Zakia.

"Well, there's my ride. I'll see you Wednesday."

"Good-bye, Julius."

Julius watched Denim as she walked away, and couldn't help but admire her curvy figure. He knew admiring her was all he could do too, since she was the girlfriend of one of the most popular guys in school. Improving his grade in algebra should be easy with a tutor as pretty as Denim.

He opened the car door and climbed in next to his father. "Hey, Dad."

"Hello, Julius. Was that your tutor walking with you?" he asked.

"Yes, sir."

He pulled away from the curb and said, "She sure is pretty. I don't know how you're going to learn anything working with her."

Julius laughed and said, "That's true, but she's actually cool. I was able to concentrate."

"Sure you were," Zakia teased her brother.

Julius rolled his eyes at his sister. "Be quiet, Zakia."

She laughed and started singing along with a Rihanna song playing on the radio.

Mr. Graham smiled and said, "Julius, you're my son, and I know you don't remember a damn thing that young lady said today."

Julius laughed.

"What's so funny?" Zakia asked.

"Nothing, sweetheart. Your brother was just telling me about one of his classmates," Mr. Graham answered. He didn't want her to know the details of his man-to-man conversation with his son, so he was vague with his response.

"Oh!" Zakia responded before she started singing along with the radio again.

Julius glanced back at his sister and then said, "She's dating André Patterson."

"The all-American?" Paul asked.

"The one and only," Julius answered. "I got a chance to meet him in the library. He was talking to me about going out for the team."

"I see. Maybe you should try out," his father suggested. "I hear he's a nice kid and that he's some type of artist too. I think I read somewhere that he's painted murals in some office buildings around town. A lot of colleges are salivating over him."

Julius changed the station on the radio and said, "He is nice, but I don't know about trying out for the team."

"What do you have to lose?"

He shrugged his shoulders and said, "Nothing I guess, but I like football a little more than basketball."

"I'm behind you one hundred percent with whatever you want to do, son. You're built for both sports, so either one would be fine."

"Thanks, Dad," he replied with a smile.

Mr. Graham pulled into their neighborhood and said, "You want to hear some good news?"

"Sure."

"I have a job interview tomorrow for a management position at the automotive plant."

"For real?" Julius asked with excitement.

"You bet, and when I get the job, we're out of here. No more gunshots in the middle of the night, and you, your mom, and your sister will be safe and sound."

"That's my dream too, Dad, because I don't think those cops are going to let up."

"What cops?" Zakia asked.

"The ones on the TV show," Julius replied to throw her off. He'd forgotten she was in the car since she'd stopped singing.

Mr. Graham put the car in park and said, "Zakia, run on in house. I want to talk to your brother for a second. We'll be in shortly."

"Okay, Daddy," she replied as she opened the car door and made her way into the house.

Mr. Graham turned to his son and asked, "Have the police tried to contact you at school?"

"No, sir, but they know I know something. I think it's only a matter of time before they try to talk to me again."

"If they do, you don't say a word. Just call me and I'll come right away. Understood?"

"Yes, sir."

"Listen, son, we haven't had a chance to talk about what happened in the store that night. Your mother told me you haven't been sleeping much. Do you want to talk about it?"

Julius laid his head on the headrest and sighed. "It's bad, Dad."

"It's okay. No matter how bad it is, I'm your father, and I'll die before I let anybody hurt you. I don't want you feeling burdened with this. What you saw was tragic and scary, and as long as the killer's on the street, I won't rest knowing you don't feel safe. You'll probably feel better if you talk about it, son."

With tears in his eyes Julius told his father exactly what had happened. He even revealed to him that it was Viper who shot the store clerk and that word on the street confirmed it was him as well. Mr. Graham knew Viper well, and so did most families in the area. He felt his blood pressure rise because of the possible threat if Viper ever found out his son was a witness.

"It doesn't surprise me that Viper was involved, because that kid's been on the fast track to nowhere for years. Julius, I'm glad you told me. That kid is dangerous, and I don't want you to tell anybody you were anywhere near that store, especially those detectives. You feel me?"

"Yes, sir."

Mr. Graham opened his car door and said, "Great. Now, don't say anything to your mother about this, because she'll really freak out. I'll tell her information on a need-to-know basis. Besides, she's worried enough already."

"I won't, Dad," Julius replied as they walked into the house to the smell of fried pork chops, macaroni and cheese, and green beans.

It was an unusually warm fall afternoon, and Detectives Daniels and Young were back in Julius's neighborhood, looking for anyone that could provide them with clues to the homicide. It wasn't the first time they had canvassed the area, and it wouldn't be the last. They knocked on doors and stopped everyone on the street for any information they could gather on the murder. On this day they parked on the corner near the store to watch the daily traffic of people going up and down the block in the hope of finding someone they hadn't already spoken to. There was one group of young men making their way down the block, bouncing a basketball, and they noticed a familiar figure in the group, so they exited their vehicle and made their way across the street in their direction.

"What's up, guys? Where are you headed? " Detective Young said to the young men.

"What's it to you?" Domingo asked.

Detective Daniels pointed at Julius and asked, "You're Julius Graham, right?"

Julius opened his mouth to answer, but nothing came out. Detective Young knew his partner had made a potentially fatal mistake by insinuating that they knew Julius.

Domingo and his friends looked at Julius, confused about how the detectives would know him, and the last thing Julius wanted his friends to think was that he was some type of informant for them.

"Julius, how do you know these cops?" Domingo asked.

Detective Young stepped forward and said, "We don't really know Julius. We found a job application with his name on it in the store where that homicide happened the other day. We asked around, and someone pointed him out to us. That's all. We're following up all leads in the case until we catch the shooter. Have you guys heard anything on the streets about the shooting?"

Domingo answered, "Hell no! You guys are crazy if you think you're going to get anyone to talk around here. We know nothing about nothing. Let's go, guys."

"We're just making conversation, kid. Chill out," Detective Daniels replied with a firm tone.

Angry at the detectives for drawing attention to him, Julius answered in anger, "You cops need to back up off me and my boys and get the hell away from us. If you keep this shit up, we're going to have the NAACP, the ACLU, and everybody else on your asses. Now stop!"

"That's right!" Domingo yelled to support his best friend.

Detective Daniels put his hands up in defense and said, "Look, we're only here to help the community. I heard Remy was good to you kids. I would think you would want to make sure the person who killed him is arrested."

Julius stepped forward and said, "What we want if is for you to leave us alone. We have to live here, and if the wrong people see us talking to you, it could get us killed."

"Forget it, Julius. These clowns don't have a clue," Domingo said to back up his friend. "We know you have snitches. Go ask them, because we're no snitches!"

With that statement, Julius, Domingo, and the other young men walked away from the detectives, leaving them empty-handed. They had hoped to scare Julius into cooperating with their investigation, but they were unsuccessful once again.

Inside the store Julius hurried over to the refrigerator and pulled out two large bottles of Gatorade and a bottle of water to purchase. His throat was dry, and he was sweating profusely. He was standing almost in the exact spot he was in the night of the shooting. All the emotions of that night came back to him like a flood, and his heart started pounding in his chest.

Domingo walked over to his friend and patted him on the shoulder, snapping him out of his trance.

"Bro, I like how you handled yourself with those bigheaded cops. They love sweating brothas."

Julius turned to his friend and said, "I know."

Domingo pulled a Gatorade out of the refrigerator and asked, "Why didn't you tell me you put in an application to work here?"

Thankful that one of the detectives was able to divert suspicion from him, he continued the lie and said, "Since my dad has been out of work, I thought it was a good place to work after school to try to help out. Too bad Remy never got a chance to hire me."

Walking toward the register, Domingo asked, "Yeah, that's too bad. So are you still going to try to work here?"

Julius sat his purchases on the countertop and said, "No way. Besides, my mom freaked when I told her I had put an application in here."

Domingo pulled his money out of his pocket and said, "Good thing you weren't working here that night, huh? You could've got shot too."

Domingo had no idea how close his statement was to the truth. The two friends paid for the Gatorade and bottled water and headed back toward the exit. When they walked outside to join their other friends, they found them occupied with a couple of girls.

Julius opened a bottle of Gatorade and said, "Looks like it's going to be a minute before we're ready to play ball."

"Those girls ain't about nothing," Domingo said before sitting down on a bench.

"My dad said as soon as he finds work, we're going to move," Julius announced.

"Move? Where?" Domingo asked.

"We don't know yet, but it'll be out of here. I'm tired of dodging bullets."

"How are we going to play ball if you move out of the neighborhood?" Domingo asked before taking a sip of Gatorade.

"We'll work it out," Julius assured him. "Come on. We have time for one more game before dark."

"Count me in!" Domingo answered as he climbed off the bench and yelled for their other friends to join them. Unfortunately, it took a few minutes, because they were working hard to get cell numbers from the girls they were talking to. After some clever begging from the guys, the girls happily scribbled out their numbers on their store receipts.

Just then Julius noticed a dark Dodge Charger coming down the street. It came to a stop right at the corner, at the stop sign. Behind the wheel of the car sat none other than Viper, and one of his boys was in the passenger seat. Just the mere sight of him made Julius extremely nervous. Viper looked over and noticed the young men hanging out outside the store, but it was Julius that he made eye contact with. Before driving off, Viper nodded at Julius, who seemed to be the only one in his group who noticed the two pull up.

"Did you see that?" Julius asked Domingo.

"What?" Domingo asked as he finished texting.

"Viper just rolled by in his car with one of his boys. Do you think somebody told him about those cops talking to us?"

"Nah. He would've come over here if he suspected anything."

Unconvinced on the inside, Julius had no choice but to hope that Domingo was right. The young men made the short walk to the basketball court and put their drinks and bags down on the bleachers. Domingo immediately threw an alley-oop pass to six foot tall sophomore Jeremy Green, who dunked it, drawing a lot of screams and high fives from spectators.

Julius glanced at the time on his cell phone and yelled, "Let's do this!"

The teens started playing the last game of the evening.

Chapter Four

Dear Diary,

School was all good today. I'm tutoring a new student named Julius. He's cute, but he's too young for me. I would introduce him to my neighbor, Kane, but she's in love. LOL! Maybe my matchmaking days are over (sigh). Anyway, he seems nice and he's very smart, but there are times when he totally shuts down on me, which leads me to believe there's something else going on with him. I don't know if he's being bullied or if there's trouble at home. Whatever's going on, I want him to see me as a friend and mentor. Who knows . . . He just might open up to me in due time. You know I'm all about helping my friends. Then again, that's what usually gets me into trouble. LOL! Well, got to go. I see my student coming.

Smooches!

D

Julius walked over to the table and slid into his seat without making eye contact with Denim. He'd been stressing ever since the shooting, and it was beginning to take a toll on him.

"Well, hello to you too," Denim said to him with an agitated tone of voice.

"Hey, Denim. Sorry," he mumbled.

She studied his expression and asked, "Are you okay?"

He sighed and said, "Yeah, I'm cool."

"Look at me," she demanded.

Julius slowly looked up at her and could see that she was not amused by his behavior, and he realized that his parents wouldn't be, either, if they saw how he was treating her. Then, just as he was about to speak, she put her hand in front of him and stood.

"Hold that thought. Our conversation needs to take place in private," she announced. "Let's go."

Stunned, Julius continued to sit.

Denim tugged on the hood of his hoodie and repeated, "I said, let's go."

Julius closed his books like a chastised child and slowly followed Denim toward the library exit. Once outside she pointed over to a picnic table underneath a row of trees near the soccer field and said, "Let's do this outside today. You seem like you need some fresh air, because your mind seems clouded."

They made their way over to the picnic table in silence and sat down across from each other. A cool breeze rustled through the leaves, and they could hear a few birds chirping in the trees nearby. It was a peaceful scene, even though Julius's emotional state was extremely tense.

"Are you ready to do some work now?" Denim asked.

"Not really, but I'll try," he answered as he looked into her concerned eyes.

She shook her head and shoved her books into her book bag. "Your mind's not in it today. Is there something you want talk about?"

"No . . . maybe," he answered in confusion.

"You're paying for the time, so it's your time whether we're doing math or whatever. Whether we're successful and meet the goal you want to meet is up to you."

Julius tapped his pencil on the table for several seconds. He looked into Denim's eyes and said, "I'm not really feeling it today, Denim. I have other stuff on my mind right now."

She sat down and asked, "Do you want to talk about it?"

He lowered his eyes and said, "Not today. I just want to chill. Is that okay with you?"

"Like I said, it's your dime, not mine. So what do you want to do?"

He smiled and said, "Can you shoot hoops?"

She stood and said, "I do okay. Is that what you want to do?"

"Yeah," he answered as he threw his book bag over his shoulders.

"Let's go over to the court. I think I have one of Dré's basketballs in my trunk."

Julius and Denim slowly make their way out to her car to get the basketball. Seconds later they began a game of horse on one end of the court, while a group of guys played three on three on the other side. After the first game, Julius started to loosen up.

"You're better than I expected you to be," Julius stated. "I guess dating a star basketball player has it perks."

Denim bounced the ball and took a shot, missing the goal.

"To tell you the truth, I could play ball before I started dating Dré. I have an older brother, and we used to play together all the time."

Julius bounced the ball and took a shot, hitting it. He turned to her and said, "I know you picked up something from being around Dré."

Denim knocked the basketball out of his hand, and while dribbling it, she said, "You underestimate my skills. I see I'm going to have to stop playing with you."

"Oh, is that what you've been doing?" he asked with a chuckle.

She took the shot from the spot where Julius had previously made his basket and got nothing but the net.

"Damn!" Julius yelled, because he had taken the shot from almost center court.

Denim put her hands on her hips before moving to another area on the court and said, "I tried to tell you. Now we're going to do this by my rules." She made a baseline shot and said, "Instead of playing horse, we're going to do algebra."

"Are you serious?" Julius asked, pouting somewhat as he dribbled the ball.

"Don't whine, Julius. Algebra is the reason we're spending time together, right?"

"Whatever," he answered as he missed his shot.

"Okay, I'm going to mix things up a little bit," she explained. "I'm going to ask you algebra questions, and if you get it right, you get to ask me questions. Get it wrong, I get to ask you other questions not pertaining to algebra. Is that fair?"

Julius was a little reluctant to agree to her terms, but he eventually decided to go along with her. Denim wasted no time asking Julius to solve algebra equations they had been studying. Some he got right, and some he got wrong. When he got a particular question wrong, Denim decided to ask him a very personal question.

"Since you missed that shot, here's your first question not related to algebra."

Julius looked at her in anticipation of the question and clenched his teeth.

"Why were so tense in the library earlier? And I want the truth, Julius Graham."

He blushed and dribbled the basketball without making eye contact with her.

"Stop stalling," Denim demanded. "You have to answer the question without hesitation."

He shot the ball and hit the shot. "I wasn't tense. It's just that I have stuff on my mind."

"What kind of stuff?" she asked, pushing him for a more direct answer. "You're not being bullied, are you?"

"No, I'm not being bullied. It's personal, and it's making it hard for me to concentrate."

Denim looked at her watch and noticed that their time together had ended and it was time to go. "We don't have a lot time to waste, Julius, so whatever you have that's messing with your head, take care of it, because report cards will be coming out soon."

He stared off across the basketball court at the other students without replying. Denim could tell he was definitely distracted, and she needed to snap him out of it. What she didn't know was how serious his distraction was.

"I'll make sure I'm on top of my game before report cards come out," he finally told her.

The last thing he wanted was to put Denim in danger, and he knew he had to be as elusive as possible.

"I hope so, because I hate that you're letting something keep you from handling your business with me," she said as she retrieved the basketball. "I'm here if you ever want to talk."

"I'll remember that, Professor."

Denim laughed.

"We'd better get going. Your dad will be looking for you at the library."

He pulled his cell phone out of his pocket and said, "It's okay. I'll text him and let him know where we are. I really had a good time today, even though it didn't start out so well."

She bumped her shoulder against his and said, "We got some work done. That's what is important, but Wednesday I'm going to come down hard on you, so you'd better be ready."

"I will," he replied as they walked toward her car.

As they walked past the guys on the other end of the court, one of them stepped out of the group and yelled out to Denim.

"Yo, Denim. Does Dré know you're kicking with that freshman?"

She put her hand out in his direction and said, "Mind your business, Tybo. This has nothing to do with you."

He ignored Denim and walked closer to get Julius's attention and started circling him like a lion sizing up his prey. "Yo, freshman! You can't be hanging out with an upperclassman's lady like this. Who do you think you are?"

Denim got between them and said, "Leave him alone, Tybo!"

Julius moved Denim to the side and said, "It's okay, Denim. I can take care of myself."

"Hey, guys, check it out. The freshman has some balls!" Tybo yelled.

Denim grabbed Julius's arm and tried to pull him toward the parking lot. "Let's go, Julius. He's not worth it."

He pulled away from her and said, "No! If I back down now, these guys will make my life here hell."

"What the hell is going on?" Dré asked. He seemed to have appeared out of nowhere. He nodded at Julius, then kissed Denim on the lips.

"Dré, I'm glad you're here, to see it for yourself. This freshman is trying to push up on your girl," Tybo proudly announced.

"That's a lie!" Denim yelled in Julius's defense.

"Hold on, babe," Dré said, interrupting her. "I want to hear what Tybo has to say. Go ahead, Tybo. Tell me how Julius pushed up on my girl?"

"Dré!" Denim yelled in disbelief. "I know you're not about to listen to this idiot."

"Chill, babe," he answered as he folded his arms. "I got this."

Tybo went on to tell Dré how Denim and Julius had been playing around on the court.

He said they were flirting and touching each other. Once he was finished, Dré turned to Julius and discreetly winked at him. Then he turned back to Tybo and gave him the verdict.

"Tybo, it's cool that you call yourself looking out for me, but you don't have to. I trust my girl, and what she's doing with my man, Julius, was strictly business. He's a cool guy, and I don't want you or anyone messing with him. Are we clear?"

Tybo laughed and said, "You didn't see what I saw."

Dré glared at Tybo and said, "Well, you're wrong, because I've been over there, under the trees, watching for the last fifteen minutes and I didn't see him do anything disrespectful."

"Whatever, Dré," Tybo replied as he waved Dré off. "Don't say I didn't try to warn you."

The trio watched as Tybo rejoined his friends on the court. Dré turned to Julius and said, "I'm glad you stood up to him. Tybo's a big guy and twice your size. You didn't back down, and I admire you for it. You might not believe it now, but he'll respect you standing up to him."

"I don't care about gaining his respect. I hate liars," Julius stated.

"Me too," Dré replied as he hugged Denim's waist and kissed her neck. "So did you guys get any work done today?"

"Julius was a little distracted today, but we were able to get a little work done."

Julius smiled and said, "I promise I'll have my head in the game at the next session."

"You'd better," she answered as they watched his dad pull up and blow the car horn.

"Well, that's my ride. I'll see you guys later."

"Have a good evening, Julius," Denim said.

He waved and ran down to his father's car and climbed in. Once he was gone, Dré picked Denim up in his arms and said, "I finally have you all to myself."

She giggled and buried her face against his warm neck and whispered, "I've missed you today."

He kissed her tenderly on the lips and said, "I've missed you too." He sat her down and asked, "Are you hungry?"

"Starving!"

"My dad's grilling. Call your parents and ask if you can come over for dinner."

She pulled out her cell phone and said, "I'm sure it'll be fine."

Dré walked Denim to her car as she got permission from her parents to have dinner with him. Once they were set, they climbed into their vehicles and trailed each other over to Dré's house.

***

Julius was quiet on the ride home to his house. His dad looked over at him and said, "Your face is red. Is everything okay?"

"How is my face red?" Julius asked as he pulled down the mirror and stared at his reflection. What he saw looking back at him was a flushed face. He had a bronze complexion and his cheeks did look a little red, but he didn't want to reveal to his father that he had almost got into a fight. So he lied.

"I was shooting ball with Denim. I guess I got a little hot."

Mr. Graham chuckled and said, "We're not paying money for you to play basketball with your tutor—"

Julius interrupted him and said, "We did study, Dad. We just did it on the basketball court."

"Okay. I just want to make sure you're serious about improving your grades and you're not wasting our money."

Julius shook his head and pulled out his cell phone to text Domingo so he could tell him about Tybo. Almost immediately Domingo texted him back. They continued to exchange messages the entire ride home, and when his father pulled into the driveway, Julius saw an unfamiliar vehicle parked there.

"Are we expecting company?" Julius asked.

Mr. Graham put the car in park and said, "No."

The two quickly climbed out of the car and hurried inside, only to find Detectives Daniels and Young waiting for them.

Chapter Five

"I thought I told you to stay away from my family," Mr. Graham yelled as he walked into the family room and found the detectives talking to his wife.

Detectives Daniels and Young stood immediately.

"Mr. Graham, it's imperative that we speak with Julius about what happened that night in the store. We're positive he knows something that could help this investigation," said Detective Daniels.

"I want you out of my house now!"

"Why is everyone yelling?" Zakia asked as she appeared suddenly from upstairs.

Mrs. Graham met her daughter at the door and said, "It's okay, baby. Go back upstairs until we finish talking to these men."

"Who are they?"

Mrs. Graham led her daughter over to the stairs and said, "They're just some men here talking about things going on in the neighborhood."

"Like what?" Zakia asked as she climbed the stairs.

"Everything," Mrs. Graham answered. "We'll talk later. Now, go do your homework." She watched her daughter disappear upstairs before rejoining everyone in the family room. When she entered the room, she saw one of the detectives talking directly to Julius.

"Julius, do you know a man called Reginald Jackson?" Detective Young asked.

Angry, Mr. Graham walked over to Detective Young and got right in his face. "If you say one more thing to my son, I won't be responsible for my actions."

"Are you threatening us?" Detective Daniels asked.

"It is what it is, Detective. You're the ones who are here harassing me and my family. Now, I'm not going to say it again."

Mrs. Graham put her arm around her son's shoulders and gave him a reassuring hug. She could see on his face that this was too much for him to bear.

"If that's the way you want it, Mr. Graham, we'll leave, but we can't guarantee that Julius won't find himself at the defendant's table or on the witness stand when this case goes to trial."

"Then looks like we'll see you in court," Mr. Graham replied before slamming the door behind them and stomping of toward the garage, which was where he normally went to think or relieve stress.

"Paul," Mrs. Graham called out to him as she and Julius followed him. "You need to calm down before you have a stroke."

Clearly agitated, he pointed his finger at Julius and said, "Son, I won't let anyone try to intimidate or hurt you. I don't care who they are, but you have to make sure you keep your mouth shut, especially to these detectives. They don't give a damn about you. All they want to do is make their case, no matter whose lives they put at risk."

"A man died, Paul," Mrs. Graham reminded him. "They wouldn't keep coming around if they didn't think Julius could help."

"They're just digging for information, Alecia. Can't you see that?" he answered as he paced the floor.

She leaned against his worktable and folded her arms.

"What I see is you stressed out and Julius scared half to death. Maybe it's time we all sat down and talk about what happened as a family so we can all be on the same page."

Julius lowered his head and nodded in agreement. At that point the three of them sat down and started talking. However, the last thing Julius wanted to do was tell his parents that the most feared man in the neighborhood was the one who killed the clerk. If they knew that he was sure, his father would pack up the family and move them out of state.

"Okay, Julius, what happened in the store that night?" Mr. Graham asked his son. "And I want the truth and nothing less."

Julius looked at his parents and said, "You guys don't want to know the truth."

"Yes, we do, son. Just talk to us," Mrs. Graham pleaded. "I'm sure you'll feel so much better once you get it off your chest."

"It's complicated," Julius whispered.

"How complicated can it be if you don't know anything?" Mr. Graham asked.

"I didn't say I didn't know anything. I said it was complicated."

Frustrated, Mr. Graham rubbed his head and said, "Those detectives are on to something, and I would feel better if I knew what happened so I'd know how to defend you. Enough bullshitting, Julius! What happened in that store, and who is Reginald Jackson?" Mr. Graham asked his son.

Julius realized he was backed into a corner and had to confide in his parents. His life was spiraling out of control.

"Dad, I feel like if I don't talk about this, it'll keep everyone safe."

Mr. Graham leaned forward and took his son by the hand and looked him in the eyes. "Son, that's not a burden you need to carry alone. We're your parents, and we're here for you."

Mrs. Graham gently cupped her son's face and stared into his eyes. "Sweetheart, your father's right. . . . Unburden yourself with this, and let us handle it. Okay?"

Feeling the pressure, Julius decided then what he thought they needed to know. "I was so scared that night, I'm not sure about anything anymore."

"That's fair, but they're targeting you for some reason. And for the last time who's Reginald Jackson?" his father asked.

"Reginald Jackson is Viper, Dad."

Mr. Graham sat up straight, because he knew exactly who Viper was, and so did everyone else in the neighborhood.

"Viper? That's the guy who's been linked to several shootings, isn't it?" Mrs. Graham asked.

"Yes, ma'am," Julius answered.

Mr. Graham stood in silence and walked across the room. He made his way over to the window and pulled back the curtain. As he looked out the window, he realized just how serious this situation had become.

"Julius?"

"Yes, sir?"

Mr. Graham turned back to his son and said, "It's a whole new ball game now. Whether Viper is the shooter or not, the detectives think he's involved. If they think he's involved and word gets out that you were in that store, it makes you a target. Was Viper the shooter, son?"

"Yes, sir," Julius answered, his voice barely above a whisper.

Mrs. Graham held her hand over her heart as she became slightly light-headed. She had heard the stories about Viper and knew what his capabilities were and understood that he wouldn't hesitate to kill her son if he thought it would keep him from going to jail. He'd been able to control the entire neighborhood by evoking fear in everyone who lived there. Now it was hitting close to home, and they had to figure out how they were going to keep the family safe.

"Okay," Mr. Graham replied. "Does anyone else know about this?"

"No, sir," Julius answered.

"Are you sure?" his father asked. "You haven't told Domingo or any of your other friends?"

"No, Dad," he answered with frustration in his voice. "No one knows."

"Good," Mr. Graham said as he pulled his son into his arms and hugged him. "Now, go on upstairs with your sister. Your mother and I need to talk about how we're going to get you out of this mess. Okay, son?"

"Okay," Julius answered. "I'm sorry, Mom."

Mrs. Graham kissed her son and said, "You have nothing to be sorry about. Just make sure to always tell us when you're in trouble so we can help."

Julius made his way toward the stairs and said, "I will. Can I go to my room now? I have a little homework to do."

Mr. Graham waved him off and said, "Go ahead, son." Once Julius was out of sight, he looked at his wife and said, "I need a drink."

"But you don't drink, baby," she answered.

"I do now."

He wrapped his arms around her waist, and she said, "Me too."

Later that evening Domingo and his eight-year-old sister, Mya, waited for their order of hot wings in a neighborhood barbecue joint. As they waited, he allowed his sister to play a game on his iPhone.

"Domingo, can I get some curly fries?"

He took his cell phone out of her hands and said, "No. You know Mom's making fries at home."

"But I like their fries," she replied as she reached for the iPhone.

"I like them too," he answered as he held the iPhone out of reach. "But Mom's making them at home, and she only gave me enough money for the wings."

Mya stared at her brother and said, "I know you have money, Domingo. You always have money."

He laughed and said, "You think you know me."

"I do know you, big brother. Besides, I always find money in your pockets."

He pointed his finger at her and said, "You'd better stay out of my pockets."

"What's wrong? Afraid I'm going to find something you're not supposed to have?"

Domingo balled up a napkin and playfully threw it at his sister just as Viper and one of his sidekicks walked through the door. In their small community, everyone pretty much knew each other, so when Viper walked in, his presence was immediately felt and it changed the atmosphere in the room.

Mya noticed everyone looking at Viper, so out of curiosity she asked, "Who's that?"

"No one you want to know," her brother answered, feeling protective.

Together they watched as Viper placed his order while his friend walked over to an old-school pinball machine and started playing.

Mya discreetly looked over her shoulder at the men. The guy at the counter was a scary-looking guy. He had a yellow bandanna showing under a black baseball cap, his hands were calloused, and he desperately needed a manicure.

"For real, Domingo, who are they?" she whispered.

Domingo leaned in close to his sister and said, "Bad men. That's who they are. Didn't you notice how a few people got up and left?"

"What did they do?" Mya whispered.

"Let's talk about this at home, sis," he replied as he looked at his ticket and wondered what was taking so long for their order to come up. It was only a twenty-piece wing order; then again, the room was pretty full, or at least it was until Viper and his boy walked in.

"Yo!" Viper yelled across the room to his friend as he pulled up his sagging pants.

"What?" his friend yelled back as the pinball machine chimed, all the bells and whistles going off.

"Are you going to order or play that damn game all day?" Viper asked with an attitude in his tone.

"Order me what I always get," he hollered back at Viper. "I'm winning here."

Viper mumbled some curse words and placed their order with the clerk. After getting his ticket, he walked over to the pinball machine and watched his friend play the game.

"Ticket number seventeen," the clerk called out over the microphone.

"That's us," Domingo said as he slid out of the booth, with Mya close behind.

As they slowly made their way up to the counter, someone burst through the door and started shooting. Domingo quickly knocked his sister down on the floor and covered her body with his as broken glass and other debris fell in the melee. Mya screamed along with many others as gunshots continued to ring out in the restaurant. Domingo was afraid to move but knew they couldn't stay where they were, so he made a quick decision, a decision that could end his life but save his sister and many others. He pushed Mya out of the line of fire into a nearby hallway.

"Domingo! What are you doing?" Mya screamed.

"Stay where you are, and keep your head down," he yelled back at his sister.

Domingo could see the shooter's legs but not his face. He was only a few feet from him and knew he was the only one in position to act, so he did. Domingo lunged for the shooter's legs and was able to tackle him to the floor, causing the gun to slide across the floor. At that moment,

Viper and his friend were able to make their way toward the exit of the restaurant, but before leaving, Viper made eye contact with Domingo. Seconds later a car was heard driving off, and they were gone as quickly as they had arrived. As far as the shooter was concerned, Domingo wasn't sure if he was still in the building, so he knew he had to get his sister out of there.

"Are you okay?" Domingo asked his sister as he checked her for injuries.

"I want to go home," she cried hysterically.

Domingo's heart was pounding in his chest as he tried to figure out how to get his sister out of there. The smell of gunpowder filled the room, and sobbing could be heard. Domingo reached for his cell phone to dial 911 but hung up when he realized it was more important to get his sister out of the building.

"I want to go home, Domingo," she sobbed even harder.

"Hang on, Mya. I'll get you out of here."

Instinct told Domingo to do whatever it took to get himself and his sister out of there. He led her into the bathroom, where he found a small window over the toilets, which he was able to get Mya through.

"Mya, don't move. I'll be right out to get you."

"Don't leave me, Domingo. I'm scared, Domingo."

"I know you are. I am too," he admitted. "Just wait for me, and if I'm not out there in five minutes, start walking home."

With tears in her eyes she nodded in agreement as she huddled down against the wall and hugged her knees. Domingo climbed down off the toilet and slowly made his way out into the hallway, where he met one of the clerks.

"What happened?" he asked the young man, who was bleeding from what appeared to be injuries from broken glass.

"Some fool came in and started shooting at Viper."

"Where is he now?" Domingo asked as he watched the young man hold a napkin over the wound on his cheek.

"I don't know. He took off out the door."

Domingo patted the young man on the shoulder and said, "Take care, bro. I have to get my sister out of here."

"I understand, bro," the clerk said as he made his way into the restroom.

Domingo cautiously exited the restaurant and turned the corner into the alley just as police cars pulled up to the curb. He grabbed Mya by the hand and basically dragged her down the alley, which ran between the restaurant and a Laundromat. Once they were at least three blocks away, they stopped to catch their breath.

Domingo hugged his sister and said, "I didn't know you could run like that."

She held on to her brother tightly and said, "Let's keep going, Domingo. We're almost home."

He tilted her chin upward and looked into her tear-streaked face and said, "I'm proud of how you handled yourself back there."

She wiped her tears and said, "I don't know why. I was screaming like a baby."

He kissed her cheek and said, "You only did what I wanted to do. Don't think I wasn't scared."

"I thought you got shot," his sister revealed.

"We're fine. I got us out of there, didn't I?" he asked. "Now your big brother is going to get you home, but I need you to pull yourself together for me. Okay?"

"I'll try," she answered. "What are we going to tell Mom and Dad?"

He took her by the hand and said, "The truth."

***

Back at the restaurant, police taped off the area, while detectives interviewed workers and the few patrons who had stuck around. As the detectives investigated the scene, they did notice a few droplets of blood leading out of the building. The droplets were pretty consistent, and it wasn't clear if they were from a bullet or flying glass.

The detectives continued questioning the manager and the counter clerks regarding the shooting, but most of them were unable to help since they had all dropped to the floor once the bullets started flying. As far as the patrons that stuck around, most of them were too afraid to get involved in the case since Viper was the obvious target in the shooting. So far none of them had even mentioned his name, and their descriptions of the face of the shooter were vague too. Since Detectives Daniels and Young had been working the homicide at the store, they drove over to the restaurant to see if this shooting was in some way related to their case.

"What happened here?" Detective Young asked the responding officers.

"We're still piecing it together," one of the officers replied. "When the shooting started, people scattered, but we still have the manager and all the employees inside."

Detective Daniels pulled out his notepad and asked, "Did anyone get hit?"

"If they did, they didn't stick around. We have officers checking area hospitals and clinics for anyone coming in with an injury consistent with a gunshot."

The detectives continued to inspect the bullet-ridden restaurant. Detective Young asked, "Does anyone know what prompted the shooting or who the target was?"

"The manager doesn't know. He said the restaurant was full when the shooting started and it's a miracle no one was killed. He also said a guy from the neighborhood they call Viper was in the restaurant before the shooting started," the officer said.

"Viper?" Detective Daniels asked. "That's a familiar name. What about the shooter? Could anyone identify him?"

"Not that we've been able to find. Witnesses said someone tackled the shooter, making him drop the gun, but whoever it was didn't stick around, either," the officer said.

"Maybe they had a good reason not to stick around," Detective Young answered. "If the restaurant has surveillance cameras, I want to see them. It could mean getting a dangerous person off the street and possibly even a killer."

Chapter Six

Denim drove home with a full stomach and a warm heart. She had enjoyed spending the afternoon with Dré and his family. The ribs were tender and delicious, and his mother's potato salad was to die for. Now she was headed home to work on a paper for her honors world history class, but before she could get there, a car barreled out of nowhere, ran the red light, and T-boned her car, sending it into a three-sixty spin. Smoke began to billow out from under the hood of Denim's car as she sat behind the steering wheel, dazed and confused. She caught a glimpse of her reflection in the mirror and noticed that her head was bleeding from a large gash. She didn't know if she had any other injuries, but after smelling smoke, she realized her car might be on fire and she went into a panic. Denim's adrenaline kicked in, and she was able to pull herself out of her Mustang. Spectators stood on the side of the road, and Denim couldn't understand why no one came to her aid.

"Could someone help me please?" she called out to them as she slowly made her way over to the car that had hit her.

Coughing from the smoke, she went to the passenger side of the car and saw a man inside, moaning in agony. The driver of the car was clearly unconscious and unresponsive.

Denim opened the passenger side door and asked, "Are you okay?"

"No. I think my leg is broken."

At that moment she heard a swooshing sound and noticed flames coming out from under the hood of the car.

"Get me out of here!" the man screamed.

"Somebody help me!" she yelled out to the large crowd that had gathered on the curb, but still no one came to her aid. Realizing no one would help her, she pulled the passenger side door open and grabbed the man's arm. "You're going to have to help me," she said. "I can't do this by myself."

The man grimaced and pushed himself out of the car as best he could while Denim pulled his upper body out of the car. Denim helped the man over to the curb and sat him down on the ground. Fire trucks and paramedics arrived on the scene and quickly doused the fire and pulled the driver out of the partially burned vehicle. He was in bad shape, but paramedics felt that he would make it.

While paramedics attended to Denim and the man she'd pulled to safety, she looked around at the crowd, glaring at them.

"It looks like you're going to need a few stitches," one of the paramedics told her.

"What about the guys who hit me?" she asked.

The paramedic looked over in the men's direction and said, "You're lucky. One of them has a broken leg, but the other one is critical and he sustained some burns."

Denim stared at the faces in the crowd and shook her head. "I need to call my parents."

At that exact moment a policeman walked over and handed Denim her purse.

"Is she going to be transported to the ER?" the policeman asked.

"I'm okay," Denim replied.

"You took a hard hit, and you need stitches. I suggest you go to make sure there are no internal injuries," the paramedic advised.

"Fine," she answered as she pulled out her cell phone and dialed her parents and then Dré. As expected, they freaked out and made a beeline to the hospital to meet her.

Minutes later Denim climbed into the back of the ambulance, alongside the man she'd helped out of the car. They made eye contact, and Denim smiled.

"How's your leg?" she asked.

"It's killing me, but the doc says I'll live," he revealed. "How about you?"

"I have a terrible headache, but other than that, I'm okay."

"Cool," he answered before closing his eyes. "What's your name, Shorty?"

"Denim," she answered. "What's yours?"

"My friends call me R.J., and by the way, thanks for helping me out of the car while everyone else stood by and watched."

"You're welcome," she answered before watching in silence as the paramedic started an IV on the man. She texted with Dré during the entire trip to the hospital, and when she stepped out of the ambulance at the hospital, her parents and Dré and his family were anxiously awaiting her arrival.

Tears filled her eyes as her parents hugged her and inspected her injury.

"I'm fine," she announced.

Dré stepped forward and gave her a hug and a kiss and said, "You don't look fine. You have blood all over your shirt."

A nurse walked over and said, "I'm sorry to break up this reunion, but we need to get her to the examining room."

Denim's mom asked, "Can I please go with my daughter?"

"Sure," the nurse replied.

Paramedics wheeled the man on a stretcher past the family, and Dré did a double take. Police also arrived to get evidence and interview the victims of the accident.

Denim's father, Samuel Mitchell, stepped forward and stopped one of the officers and asked, "Was that man the one who hit my daughter?"

"Who's your daughter, sir?"

"Her name is Denim Mitchell. She was driving a Mustang."

The officer looked at his notes and said, "Yes, she was hit by another vehicle. The man they just brought in was the passenger of the vehicle. The driver of the car has already been brought in, in critical condition."

"Was alcohol involved?" Mr. Mitchell asked curiously.

"Our investigation is still in the preliminary stage, but we didn't see any evidence of any at the scene," the officer revealed. "Once we have more information, I'll make sure it's passed on to you and your family."

In the examination room, Valessa Mitchell held her daughter's hand while the doctor checked Denim for various injuries. Once he finished with the first round of tests, he turned to Denim and asked her if it was okay to discuss her medical situation in front of her mother. Denim nodded in confusion, not understanding the repercussions. That was when the doctor explained that since she was eighteen, she had the right to privacy regarding her medical condition. With that behind them, the doctor exited the room and allowed the nurse to continue with Denim.

"Okay, Denim, after we stitch up that cut on your head, the doctor would like you to go for a few X-rays just to rule out any unseen injuries, but before we take you up, I also need to verify whether or not there's a possibility that you could be pregnant."

Denim's eyes widened and her skin unexpectedly changed color and so did her mother's.

She cleared her throat and said, "Well, there's a possibility, but I'm pretty sure I'm not."

"Denim," Mrs. Mitchell whispered.

"Mom, don't start. I'm careful," Denim revealed. "What do you want me to do? Lie?"

Her mother shook her head and immediately teared up.

Seeing Mrs. Mitchell's anxiety, the nurse intervened and said, "Mrs. Mitchell, it's never easy finding out your children are sexually active, but at eighteen, it is a reality, and I commend your daughter for being honest. I have no doubt that you've given Denim all the right tools to become a responsible young woman."

With that said, Mrs. Mitchell cupped her daughter's face, kissed her cheek, and said, "I love you, and I trust you'll continue to make good choices. Don't let me down."

"Don't worry, Mom. I won't," Denim replied before getting into the wheelchair so she could go get her stitches and X-rays.

Mrs. Mitchell wiped the stray tears from her eyes and said a silent prayer that God would continue to protect her daughter, watch over her, and help her make sound decisions regarding her future.

An hour or so later Denim was dismissed from the hospital with a clean bill of health, aside from having a slight concussion and some bruising. She was told that her muscles would probably be sore for a couple of days but otherwise she was okay. During the ride home, she pulled her diary out of her purse and made a short notation.

> *Dear Diary,*
> *I freaked out my parents and Dré again today. I feel like I have an invisible target on my chest or something. Got in an accident, and now I'm a little banged up. My car is probably totaled, but it could've been much worse. Angels were definitely watching over me once again. My head is throbbing from a gash on it, and I have a slight concussion. I can't wait to get home so I can lie down. Not sure if I'm going to go to school tomorrow.*
> *D*

Denim slept for the rest of the afternoon and all night. When she woke up the following morning and sat on the side of the bed, she couldn't believe how sore her body was. As she looked in the mirror, she noticed bruises that weren't on her body the day before. That was when she realized that she'd gone through more trauma than she'd originally thought, and there was no way she could go to school today or tutor Julius. Luckily, her work schedule was only part-time this time of year. However, her cheerleading schedule was full-time, causing her to miss their grueling practices for a few days.

A soft tap on her bedroom door interrupted her thoughts. She opened the door to find her mother standing on the other side with a heating pad, toast, and some orange juice.

"How are you feeling?" Mrs. Mitchell asked as she sat the tray on the nightstand.

"Sore. Thanks for the heating pad."

Mrs. Mitchell sat down in the chair next to her daughter's bed and asked, "You're not trying to go to school, are you?"

She leaned down and showed her mother the bruises on her arm and leg. "No, ma'am. Look at these bruises. I didn't have them yesterday."

Mrs. Mitchell ran her hand over her daughter's soft skin and said, "It doesn't surprise me.

I'm sure it'll be a couple of days before you're feeling more like yourself."

Denim climbed back into bed and said, "I need to call Julius and cancel my tutoring sessions with him until further notice."

Her mother stood and said, "Go ahead and eat that toast so you can take your meds. All you need to do is rest. A little later you can get in our jetted tub to help soothe your muscles."

Denim nodded as she bit into the toast.

Her father poked his head in the door and said, "How's the patient this morning?"

"I'm fine, Daddy."

He kissed her forehead and said, "Dré stopped by on his way to school. He's having a fit about getting to see you."

"He's here now?" Denim asked before jumping out of bed and sprinting into the bathroom to brush her teeth and wash her face.

Mrs. Mitchell smiled and then turned to her husband and said, "I see she's not that sore, after all. Go downstairs and stall him for a few minutes, until she get herself together. I'll let you know when she's presentable."

"Okay, boss," he replied before giving his wife a kiss on the lips.

***

Julius leaned against his locker, reading his text messages. One in particular caught his attention. It was a text from Denim about canceling their tutoring session. Her text informed him that she had been in a car accident but that she was okay, just sore from the ordeal. Concerned, he quickly dialed her number and waited for her to answer. When he heard her voice, he felt immediate relief. He had become quite attached to Denim and saw her as a dear friend. She assured him over and over that she was fine and told him she would give him all the info on her ordeal in a day or two. Satisfied, Julius wished her well and made a mental note to send her flowers after school.

"Julius!" Domingo called out to his best friend. "Why haven't you returned my call?"

Julius tucked his cell phone in his pocket and said, "Life's been kind of crazy. Those detectives showed up at my house again, and my dad went ballistic."

"Why are they sweating you so hard just because your job application was in the store?"

"I don't know," Julius replied.

"Well, forget them. I was watching *Law & Order* one time, and the cops kept doing that to a lady, and she filed a harassment complaint against them. Your parents might need to think about doing something like that."

"Maybe so," Julius answered right before a girl from his science class walked over and gave him a hug.

"Hey, Citra," Julius greeted her with a mischievous grin.

"Hi, Julius," she said as she caressed his arm.

Julius gave Citra a tight hug and said, "What's up, girl?"

Citra then turned to Domingo and greeted him with a teasing tone. "Hello, superhero. Do you have a big *S* on your chest under that shirt?"

Confused, Julius asked, "Why are you calling him a superhero?"

"Oh, you haven't heard about our little hero?" Citra asked. She gave Julius another hug and, before walking off, said, "I'll let him tell you. See you in the cafeteria."

After Citra walked away, Julius asked, "Superhero?"

"That's why I was blowing up your phone," Domingo stated. "You're not going to believe what happened to me yesterday."

They started walking down the hallway together, but Julius stopped in his tracks when

Domingo told him about Viper and what happened at the barbecue joint.

"You got caught up in a shoot-out? Tell me your bullshitting me."

"Hell, no, I'm not bullshitting," Domingo replied. "It was like the Wild, Wild West up in there, bro. I don't know who that fool was that was shooting at Viper, but he meant business, whoever he was. Since Mya was with me, I knew I had to do something."

"I still can't believe you tackled the guy. You could've gotten your ass shot," Julius stated.

It was still a minute or two before the bell was scheduled to ring, so they stood outside their classroom and continued to talk about what had happened.

"All I was thinking about was keeping my ass alive so I could save my sister. I wouldn't have been able to live if she had got hit," Domingo said as the bell rang. "Look, I'll tell you more after school."

"Maybe later. My tutor, Denim, was in a car accident yesterday, and I want to take her some flowers or something," Julius revealed.

"Is she okay?" Domingo asked.

"She said she was a little sore but otherwise okay. I'll know more after I see her."

The pair gave each other a handshake and agreed to finish their conversation later.

After school Julius hurried out the door to the bus loading area so he could catch his bus. Dré spotted him rushing down the stairs and called out to him.

"Hey, Dré. I'm sorry, but I can't talk right now. I have to catch my bus."

Dré grabbed him by the back of his jacket, stopping him, and said, "Slow down, young-blood. I can take you home. I want to holler at you for a sec."

Out of breath, Julius asked, "Are you sure?"

"Yeah, I'm sure," Dré answered as he stood there with a couple of friends. "Just call your parents and make sure it's okay."

Julius quickly pulled out his cell phone and dialed his father, who gave him permission to ride with Dré, but he also gave him a short lecture on being responsible. Once the call was over, he hung up and said, "My dad said it was okay. Thanks."

"Great!" Dré replied as they walked toward the parking lot. "Did you hear that Denim was in a car accident?"

Julius sighed and said, "She sent me a text this morning. I called to make sure she was okay. Is she really okay?"

Dré deactivated his car alarm and opened the door.

"She's pretty banged up, but she's fine. I'm getting ready to go by there, so I thought you might want to ride with me."

Julius climbed into the passenger side of the car and said, "My plan was to take her some flowers, anyway. I hope you don't mind stopping by the store so I can pick some up."

Dré smiled and said, "Of course I don't mind. Let's go."

Chapter Seven

"Denim! You have company!" her mother yelled from downstairs.

"Is it Dré?" she yelled back.

"No, it's not. Just get down here, sweetheart." Mrs. Mitchell smiled at Denim's guest as they waited for her in the foyer.

When Denim finally appeared, she couldn't believe her eyes. "R.J.? What are you doing here? Aren't you supposed to be somewhere with your leg elevated?"

Denim led R.J. into the family room as he replied, "I didn't break my driving foot."

Mrs. Mitchell followed them into the room and said, "I'm sure the doctors told you to take it easy, though."

He sat down and laid his crutches on the floor. "They did, but I'm hardheaded."

Denim giggled as she sat on the sofa and curled her legs underneath her body. "Are you in any pain?" she asked.

"A little, but the pain pills help," he replied. "I just wanted to come by to apologize about totaling your car and to see how you were doing."

Denim held out her arms and showed off a couple of bruises and said, "I'm a little bruised, but I'll be fine."

R.J. reached into his pocket and pulled out a thick envelope and gave it to her. "I also wanted to thank you again for saving my life. I could've burned up in that car if you hadn't gotten me out."

"What's this?" Denim asked as she slowly opened the envelope and pulled out a stack of money. "I can't accept this," she announced as she put the money back in the envelope and handed it back to him.

"She's right," Mrs. Mitchell added as she glanced inside the envelope. "Denim did what anyone would do."

"That's the point, Mrs. Mitchell. Denim was the only one who did do something. Everyone else was content to stand on the curb and watch me burn to death," he replied. "Besides, her car is damaged, and it's my responsibility to make sure it's repaired or replaced."

"That's true, but I think that is more than enough to replace Denim's car," she answered.

"There has to be at least ten thousand dollars in there. We can't accept this."

"If my suspicions are correct, you're probably losing time from work by staying at home with Denim. I'm sure Denim's losing time from school and maybe a job herself. It would make me feel better if you would let me do this for you," R.J. explained.

Mrs. Mitchell took the envelope out of Denim's hand and said, "I'm not concerned about losing time from work, but we appreciate you offering to pay for her car. If there's anything left over, we'll make sure it's returned to you."

R.J. reached for his crutches. "No need. Put it in Denim's college fund or something."

Denim helped R.J. up from his seat and said, "It was really nice of you to come all the way over here to see me."

He put the crutches under his armpits and said, "I wouldn't have it any other way. I hope you're feeling better soon."

"You too," Denim replied as she and her mother walked him to the door.

When Mrs. Mitchell opened the door, they were met by Dré and Julius on the porch.

"Hey, guys," Denim greeted happily.

Julius couldn't speak. He was in shock, and so was Dré.

"This is R.J. He came by to see how I was doing," Denim explained. "R.J., this is my boyfriend, Dré, and my friend Julius."

R.J. held his hand out to the boys, and when he shook Julius's hand, he asked, "What's up, li'l man? I know you, don't I?"

Julius shrugged his shoulders and stuttered, "I—I don't know. I mean, maybe."

"I've seen you around the neighborhood and playing ball in the park. Yeah, I know you," R.J. said. "You're a good kid. Make sure you stay in school and away from all the craziness in the street."

"Great advice," Denim answered.

R.J. shook Dré's hand and said, "Everybody knows you, man. You're a hell of a ballplayer, and you made me a lot of money last year. I can't wait until the season starts this year."

"Thanks," was all Dré could say as he walked past R.J. Then he mumbled something under his breath.

Julius nervously followed him into the house, with his head hanging. Denim looked at them curiously and wondered why they were acting so strangely. She decided to discuss it with them once R.J. was gone.

"You don't have to walk me to my car, Denim. I got it. Go back inside with your guests."

"Good-bye, R.J., and drive safely."

"I will," he replied, then walked to his car, threw his crutches in, and climbed inside.

Denim reentered the house and found Dré and Julius talking to her mother in the family room.

"What the hell was that?" she asked them as she joined them in the family room. "I know you two have manners. Why did you treat R.J. like that?"

Mrs. Mitchell exited the room and said, "Watch your language, young lady."

Once her mother was out of the room, Denim folded her arms and said, "I'm waiting."

Dré walked over to her and asked, "Why was that man in your house?"

"What are you talking about?" she asked. "That's R.J. He was the passenger in the car that hit me, and he came to thank me for getting him out of the burning car and to see how I was doing. Oh, and he also gave me some money to fix my car."

Dré shook his head in disbelief. He turned to Julius and said, "You know who he is, right?"

Julius nodded in silence because Denim and Dré didn't know the half of what he knew.

"Denim, you might know him as R.J., but that's Viper!" Dré revealed. "He's bad news, and he's dangerous. Stay away from him."

"He doesn't seem dangerous to me. Actually, he's really nice," she insisted. "What has he done? Killed somebody?"

Julius's heart skipped a beat because he knew for a fact that Viper had killed someone, and that was only the victim he knew about.

Dré walked over to Denim, clearly frustrated. "Denim, he's tied to drugs, gangs, murder. You name it, he's done it. If your parents knew what we know, they would go ballistic."

Denim looked at Julius and asked, "You know about him too?"

"Yeah, I know of him. Dré is right. He's bad news."

Denim sat down and finally noticed the flowers in Julius's hands. She smiled and asked, "Are those for me?"

Julius snapped himself out of a trance and handed her the flowers. "Yes, they're for you. I hope I didn't ruin them by squeezing the stems to death. Seeing Viper at your house kind of messed me up."

"I didn't know," she said as she sank down on the sofa, stunned by all the information.

"Well, now you do," Dré replied. "And if he comes around again, let me know and I'll handle it. He needs to know that he's not wanted or needed around here."

"Dré's right about that," Julius added. "There are people who want him dead. You can't afford to get caught in the cross fire. Somebody took a shot at him in a crowded restaurant yesterday."

"Yesterday?" Dré asked. "What time?"

"I'm not sure. It was sometime yesterday afternoon. My friend Domingo and his sister were there when it happened."

"Maybe that's where he was coming from when they T-boned you," Dré stated.

"Okay, you two," Denim said. "Calm down. It's in the past now."

Dré sat down and put his arm around the love of his life and said, "Yes, it is because I don't want you nowhere near that man."

"I'm, talking crazy," she said as she waved Dré off. "No, we're going together."

"Julius, you sure are quiet," Dré asked. "Are you okay?"

Julius rubbed his eyes and sat down in a nearby chair and then said, "Not really."

Concerned, Denim asked, "What's wrong?"

"Yeah, li'l bro, what's up? You know you can talk to us."

With tears in his eyes, Julius said, "Not on this one. It's too deep."

"Wait a minute," Denim said, as if a lightbulb had gone off in her head. "Has Tybo been bullying you again?"

"Nah, it has nothing to do with him," he replied. "Look, just forget I said anything."

"A look like that is hard to forget," Denim answered as she put her flowers in a vase filled with water. "I don't want to pressure you into talking, but if someone's bothering you or you're in some kind of trouble, you need to tell someone."

Julius smiled to try to break the tension in the room. "I'll keep that in mind, Professor."

"Since you have jokes, don't you have a test coming up?" she asked.

"Yes. Day after tomorrow," he revealed as he stood.

"You'd better be studying for it."

Julius smiled and said, "I am. Dré, I'd better be getting home. I hope you feel better soon, Denim."

She hugged his neck and said, "I will. Thanks again for the flowers. Now, go home and study."

Dré gave Denim a kiss and said, "I'll be back shortly. I have to run Julius home."

Denim settled in on the sofa with her laptop and said, "Take your time."

When Dré returned to Denim's house thirty minutes later, he found Denim in the family room, still surfing the Web.

He sat down next to her and asked, "What are you doing?"

Without making eye contact, she said, "Googling information on R.J."

"Why?"

"I need to see it for myself," she answered. "What's his real name?"

Dré shook his head in disbelief. "Do you really want to know the truth? Because I don't think you can handle the truth," he said in his Jack Nicholson impersonation from the movie *A Few*

Good Men as he tossed a sofa pillow in the air like a basketball.

Denim giggled. "Seriously, what's his name?"

He sat down beside her and let out a breath. "Are you sure you want to know?"

"Yes. Now, for the last time what's his name?"

"Reginald Jackson."

Denim typed in the name and watched as the search engine brought up article after article with Reginald Jackson's name included in it. There were news reports of some of the worst crimes imaginable, and Denim couldn't believe her eyes.

She closed the lid on her laptop and turned to Dré. "Okay, I get it. Are we cool?"

He gently kissed the bruise on her shoulder and then her lips and said, "You're more than cool with me, Cocoa Princess."

Dré continued to kiss her, this time more passionately, until they were interrupted by Mrs. Mitchell clearing her throat.

"You must be feeling better," she said to her daughter, who was startled by the interruption and jumped away from Dré.

"Yes, ma'am."

Dré blushed and said, "Sorry about that, Mrs. V."

She sat down across from the young couple and stared directly at Dré.

"I appreciate you apologizing, Dré, but I was young once, so I understand what it's like to be young and in love. What I do want to reiterate with you two is that you have to be extremely careful with the choices you make because your futures are at risk, and I'll leave it at that," she said, then stood and walked out of the room.

Dré's eyes were as big as basketballs. He was totally caught off guard by Mrs. Mitchell's comment. "What was that all about?"

Denim took his hand in hers and said, "She knows we're having sex."

He covered his face with his hands in disbelief. "You're kidding, right?"

"No, I'm not. I had to tell her. We were in the emergency room and the nurse was asking me all these questions and one of the questions was if I could possibly be pregnant. I couldn't lie."

He put his arm around her shoulders and said, "Well, you can forget about ever doing it again. They're not going to let me take you anywhere now."

Mrs. Mitchell walked back into the room and asked, "Dré, are you staying for dinner?"

He looked over at Denim, who was nodding her head.

"Yes, ma'am, if it's okay with you."

She waved him off and as she exited the room she said, "Of course it's okay. Just call your parents to get their approval."

"Okay, Mrs. V.," he answered as he pulled out his cell phone and sent his parents a text.

"Why don't you think they'll let me go anywhere with you?" she asked.

"Come on, Denim. Every time you walk out the door, they're going to think we're going somewhere to get busy."

She snuggled up to him and said, "And what would be so wrong with that? I wish we could go somewhere right now."

"Please! You're already bruised up from the accident. I would only do more damage, so get that thought out of your head."

Denim giggled and then kissed him seductively on the neck and whispered, "I can't wait."

He looked over at her and studied her expression. She had that yearning look on her face. He caressed her cheek and said, "Okay, let's take a ride. My parents are not home, so we can . . ."

Denim's eyes widened just before he received a text, which snapped the young couple out of their sensual trance.

He read the text and said, "I can stay for dinner. Are you ready to go?"

"My mom is not going to let me go anywhere right now."

He stood and said, "Yes, you can. Let me handle it. You started it, and now I'm going to finish it."

Dré alerted Mrs. Mitchell of his parents' approval to stay for dinner before asking her permission to take Denim over to the salvage yard to get her book bag out of her wrecked car.

"Can't this wait? I could call your father to see if he could pick it up on his way home from work," Mrs. Mitchell stated.

"It'll be closed by the time Daddy gets there. We won't be gone long," Denim replied as she kissed her mother and slid into her jacket.

Mrs. Mitchell walked the couple to the door. As she watched them walk down the sidewalk, she said, "Dré, drive carefully with my baby."

He smiled and said, "I will. Do you need anything while we're out?"

She thought for a second and said, "You can pick up some dessert if you want to."

"Yes, ma'am," he answered before he closed Denim's door and then climbed into his car and backed out of the driveway.

Dré looked at the time on his cell phone and said, "We don't have much time, so we need to take care of business before pleasure."

Denim couldn't believe she was actually going through with this mischievous plan with her boyfriend, but the excitement of it made it hard for her to restrain herself. She sat in the car while Dré ran into the store to pick up dessert. He came out with a delicious-looking carrot cake and placed it on the backseat.

"How are we doing on time?" he asked his passenger.

"We're good."

He placed his hand on her thigh and asked, "Are you sure you're up for this?"

"After what I just went through, you bet."

He kissed her and then said, "I love you."

"I love you more," she replied as he pulled out of the parking lot.

It took about ten minutes to get to the salvage yard. It was the first time Dré had an opportunity to see the destruction of Denim's car. As he stared at it, he was amazed that she wasn't killed. He pulled her into his arms and hugged her tightly.

"Looks bad, huh?" she said as she looked up into Dré's eyes.

He kissed the top of her head and said, "Yes, it does. Angels were definitely watching over you that day. Let's get your bag and get out of here."

Dré reached inside the mangled car and pulled her book bag and jacket off the front seat. He also got all her personal information out of the glove compartment before leaving the salvage yard.

By the time they made it to Dré's house, they had been on the road approximately thirty-five minutes. Hand in hand they entered the quiet house and Dré's room, where he closed his bedroom door and locked it.

"Are you sure your parents won't walk in on us?" she asked nervously.

"I'm sure. They're at their second home," he joked.

"They're at the casino?" she asked.

He placed his keys on the dresser and nodded in silence. Denim proceeded to shed her jeans and shirt, and when Dré saw just how bruised and battered her body was, he took a step back and said, "I can't do this."

She walked over to him and said, "It's not as bad as it looks. I'm okay, seriously."

Dré rubbed his neck as he contemplated what he was about to do. Seeing how reluctant he was, she took his hand in hers and caressed it. Dré had always loved her hand massages, especially before big basketball games, because they had a warm, soothing effect on him.

"The clocks ticking, prime time," she whispered in his ear. "Are you up for this or not?"

It had been a while since she had called him by his nickname, and hearing it helped him let go of any apprehension he was having. So, after careful thought, he disrobed, exposing himself, as bare as a newborn baby, and over the next twenty minutes they intimately confessed their love for one another. It was overwhelming for Dré, who thought he had lost her forever, so he made a point to kiss each and every one of her bruises. Denim relished the waves of passion flowing over her.

Dré kissed her soft lips and whispered, "I can't wait to marry you."

She looked him in the eyes and said, "As soon as we both graduate college, I'm all yours."

Tears formed in Dré's eyes because he knew Denim was the woman he wanted to spend the rest of his life with. If he could marry her right now, he would, but he had promised his parents that he would wait. The problem was that he had no idea which college he was going to end up at, making it unlikely that he and Denim would be together during that time. He kissed her once more and then stared at the ceiling.

"We'd better go, before your mom does a drive-by."

She noticed the look of sadness in his eyes, so she cupped his face and said, "Whatever you're worrying about, let it go. I love you, and you love me. Everything's going to be okay."

He smiled and said, "You're right, babe. Let's get out of here."

Julius lay across his bed, still in shock over coming face-to-face with Viper. He had nearly peed on himself when their eyes met. He felt like Viper was reading his thoughts and would figure out that he had seen him shoot the store clerk. Julius feared that Denim could get hurt because of her association with Viper. He'd found out that a lot of people had witnessed her helping Viper out of the burning car and they were pissed. They didn't care that she was a Good Samaritan. All they cared about was that Viper was still going to be roaming the neighborhood, doing the callous things he was already suspected of doing. He just prayed that nobody would take their anguish out on Denim, whom he had come to care for very much. Then there was the man who was gunning for Viper at the restaurant. He was still out on the streets, and Julius knew that this man wouldn't think twice about taking another shot at Viper, no matter where he was. Now, staring down at his math book, he found it hard to concentrate, but he couldn't let his tutor down by failing the algebra test coming up. He would have to push through all the drama on his mind so he could get an A on that test.

Chapter Eight

A few days later Julius and Domingo sat outside talking to friends as they waited on their bus. Julius proudly glanced down at the B-plus he had received on his algebra test and then waved it in Domingo's face. Denim was feeling much better and had returned to school. She saw Julius and Domingo when she exited the school, so she walked over to them and sat down beside them.

"So I hear you got your test back. Did you pass?" she asked Julius.

With a huge smile on his face, he held the test up to her and said, "B-plus!"

Denim took the test out of his hand and said, "I knew you could do it! I'm so proud of you."

Just then, a couple of guys walked past them. One stopped for a moment and then reached into his book bag.

He turned to Denim and said, "Since you like rescuing vipers so much, here's another one."

The boy tossed the item into Denim's lap and took off running. Startled, all three of them jumped up and realized that he had thrown a snake at her.

Denim screamed as she watched the critter slither toward some nearby bushes.

"Son of a bitch!" Domingo yelled as he backed away from the snake.

"Did it bite you?" Julius asked as he checked Denim for bite marks.

She shook her head and said, "No, I don't think so."

Domingo yelled for someone to get a school resource officer. When the officer arrived, he found out what happened and then took his baton and searched the bushes.

"Did anyone see what kind of snake it was or who threw it?" he asked as he continued to search for the snake.

There were a lot of kids standing around, but no one spoke up to help the officer. Some were laughing, and others were shaking their head in disbelief. The officer finally found the snake, and he and a science teacher were able to determine that it was harmless before putting it in a large container.

The officer approached Denim, who was clearly trembling, to make sure she was okay. Once he determined she was, he asked, "What really happened out here?"

Domingo spoke up and said, "We were just sitting here, chilling, and some fool walked by and tossed that snake at her."

The officer pulled out his notebook and asked, "Who did it?"

"I didn't get a look at him. All I saw was the snake," Denim admitted.

"What about you?" the officer asked Domingo.

"I'm scared of snakes. Hell, I ran," he revealed.

Julius knew exactly who had done it and he planned to handle it himself, so when the officer asked him the same question, he lied and said that he saw the guy only from behind as he ran away. He told him he was too busy trying to make sure Denim was okay. The officer closed his notebook and told them that if they remembered anything to let him know as soon as possible. As he left, he made the crowd disperse, leaving the three standing there, trying to understand what had just happened.

Domingo turned to Julius and said, "You heard what that dude said, right?"

Julius picked up Denim's book bag and said, "Yeah, I heard him."

"What did he say?" Denim asked nervously. "Was it directed at me?"

"Don't worry about it, Denim," Julius replied. "I know what this is about, and I'm going to handle it."

She grabbed his arm and said, "No, you're not. If you know something, you need to tell me!"

Julius thought about it for a moment and said, "No, I'm tired of walking around here, not knowing what's going to happen next. Domingo, let's go."

"Where are you going?" Denim asked, but her question fell on deaf ears as she watched Julius and Domingo walk out of the school yard and down the block.

Once they got a block away from the school, Domingo looked over at his friend and asked, "What are you going to do?"

"I don't know, but I have to do something," he replied.

They climbed on the city bus and made their way back to their neighborhood. When they hopped off the bus, all Julius could think about was how scared Denim was when she saw that snake. When they reached the neighborhood store on the corner of Elk, they saw a group of young men standing on the corner. Julius recognized one of them, and a sudden wave of anger immediately hit him. He dropped his book bag and sprinted over to the young men and jumped on one of them and repeatedly punched him in the face. The other guys tried to pull Julius off of the young man, but Domingo intervened, warning them to stay back. He wasn't sure why his best friend had jumped on the guy, but whatever the reason he was going to back him up and make sure he didn't get ganged up on by the others. Julius continued to beat the young man until they heard a car come to a screeching halt.

A man jumped out and pulled Julius off and yelled, "Get the hell off my brother!"

Domingo jumped in and shouted, "Get off my partner!"

The man pulled out a gun and said, "Back the hell up, youngblood!"

Domingo couldn't believe his eyes. He recognized the man, who appeared to be in his mid- to late twenties.

Julius was still angry, so angry that he wasn't aware that the man was pointing a gun at him.

"Julius, chill," Domingo whispered.

"I'm not chilling," Julius muttered. He faced the man with a gun. "Your brother threw a snake on a friend of mine. What kind of bullshit is that?"

The man smiled and then looked over at his little brother and asked, "Did you do that?"

"Yeah, I did it," the young man replied as he wiped the blood running down his nose. "I threw it on that bitch that helped Viper out of that burning car."

The man looked at Julius, and with a scowl on his face, he asked, "What is that girl to you?"

Breathing hard, Julius said, "She a friend, and she had nothing to do with Viper. She didn't even know who he was when she helped him."

"Is that so?" the man asked as he put the gun back in his waistband and folded his arms.

Julius stood toe-to-toe with him and said, "Hell, yes, it's so. I don't know what kind of beef you have with Viper, but I want you to leave my friend out of it!"

The man smiled and then said, "You have a lot of heart to jump my little brother like this. All right, I believe you."

"He's lying, Rock!" the young man yelled.

"No, I'm not!" Julius yelled back. "She's not that kind of girl. She's not from the hood."

The man put his hand up to silence his brother. He looked at Julius and said, "Like I said, you don't have to worry about your friend anymore. She must be cool if you would risk your neck over her like this."

"She *is* cool," Julius stated as Domingo handed him his book bag.

"Get in the car, bro," the man instructed his brother before they pulled away from the curb, just as a police cruiser eased down the block.

Domingo pulled Julius by the arm and said, "That's the guy."

"What guy?" Julius asked.

"That's one of the guys that shot at Viper at the barbecue joint, so you know he wouldn't think twice about shooting your skinny ass."

"Are you serious? This is getting too crazy."

"You could've been killed, dude. When I saw that gun, I thought that was it."

"I know, but I can't worry about Viper anymore or that guy, Rock, or whatever his name is."

Domingo grabbed his arm and asked, "What do you mean, you can't worry about Viper?"

Julius stared up at the sky as he fought to keep his secret.

Domingo punched him in the arm playfully and yelled, "Talk to me, bro! We've been friends since we were little kids. Whatever it is, I got your back."

Julius looked over at his best friend and said, "It's nothing."

"You're lying, and you know I can tell when you're lying. You haven't been yourself for a few weeks now. Talk to me!"

Julius felt overwhelmed. He didn't know if it was because the detectives wouldn't leave him alone or if it was because the guy had thrown a snake on Denim or even if it was because he had been up close and person with Viper. Whatever it was, he was fed up and ready to rid himself of all the anxiety he was holding in.

He grabbed Domingo by the sleeve of his jacket and said, "Follow me."

Domingo followed Julius down the block and over to the park. When they reached the bleachers at the basketball court, Domingo sat down and Julius started pacing up and down the bleachers.

"What's up?" Domingo asked again.

Julius took a breath and said, "Bro, can I trust you, and I mean really trust you?"

"Of course you can."

"I'm serious, Domingo. This is some real shit I'm about to tell you, and you can't repeat a word of what I'm about to tell you."

Domingo put his hands over his head and said, "Will you just say it already?"

Julius sat down on the bleachers next to Domingo and whispered, "I know who killed Remy."

"Everybody knows who did it. Tell me something I don't know," Domingo joked.

Julius mumbled, "Well, I know who did it because I was there."

Domingo's face suddenly faded to a pale shade, and he mumbled, "What?"

Julius looked Domingo in the eyes and said, "I was there. I saw Viper shoot Remy."

"Get the hell out of here!"

"You know I wouldn't joke about something like this," he replied. "We're talking about Viper. I almost pissed on myself when I ran into him at Denim's house."

"Denim's house? Why was he at Denim's house?"

"He came by to pay her for the damage to her car. He was in the car that T-boned her the other day."

"Wait a second. That had to have been the same day those fools shot up the barbecue joint. She's lucky she didn't get killed."

"I know. Denim didn't have a clue who he was. Her boyfriend, Dré, almost went ballistic."

Domingo was speechless. He had no idea his best friend had been carrying this burden around all this time. "If Viper finds out you saw him, you're as good as dead," he finally said.

Julius picked up his book bag and said, "Exactly! That's why I'm ready for this to be over, one way or another."

"What are you going to do now?" Domingo asked as he followed his friend toward the park exit.

"I'm trying to figure that out. Those detectives have been sweating me. I don't want to be a snitch, but Remy was cool and didn't deserve to go out like that, and it's only a matter of time before he does it again."

"Yeah, unless that dude who shot at him finds him first."

Julius stopped in his tracks and said, "That's my out."

"How the hell can that be your out?" Domingo asked.

"You'll see. I have to go!" Julius said to his friend. Then, as he walked slowly down the block, he called back, "Remember you promised not to say a word to nobody."

"Okay! Okay! I'll text you later."

Julius continued to walk down the block toward his house. His mind was going in a hundred directions as he tried to figure out how to get out of this situation. Then he figured the best thing for him to do was to face his fears head-on, deal with them once and for all. So when the bus pulled up to the curb, he got on and settled into a seat for the short ride that would take him to the other side of the neighborhood and into enemy territory. He sat next to an older gentleman who was reading a newspaper. Julius looked down and noticed his dirty shoes. He wondered what kind of work he did or if he worked at all. He looked at his hands, and they looked callous and tired.

The man caught Julius looking at him and asked, "You have something you want to ask me, son?"

"No, sir. I was just wondering where you work. I've been looking for a job."

The man closed his newspaper and said, "Is that so? Tell me, son, what do you know how to do?"

"Well, I can do almost anything if someone trains me."

The gentleman laughed and said, "I hear that. What's your name?"

"Julius Graham," he answered.

The man shook Julius's hand and said, "It's nice to meet you, Julius. My name is Frank McElroy. How old are you?"

"I'm fourteen," Julius admitted.

"You're a little young, but I'm glad you're willing to work. Most of these young cats around here don't want to do nothing but rob, steal, or sell drugs. It's good to meet a kid who's willing to work for his money. Your parents raised you right."

"Thank you."

"Okay, Julius. If it's okay with your parents and it won't affect your schoolwork, I have a job for you."

Julius eyes widened with excitement. "Yes, sir, I would love a job. What do you do?"

"I do landscaping for most of the business complexes in the city. I have a little shop in Arrington. It's hard work, but it's honest work."

"You don't own a car?" Julius asked.

He smiled and said, "I do, but I take the bus three days a week to conserve gas and to help the environment. What about you? Are you going to be able to do this in the afternoons and some weekends?"

"I have to talk to my parents, but I should be able to."

The bus stopped, and the man stood and gave Julius his business card. "Give me a call after you talk to your parents, and we can work out a schedule for you."

With a smile on his face, Julius took the card and said, "Thank you, Mr. McElroy."

He shook Julius's hand and said, "I look forward to hearing back from you."

Julius watched Mr. McElroy get off the bus and walk down the block. He stared at the card and hoped that this was a sign of his luck changing for the better, then tucked it inside his book bag and got back to the business at hand. Three stops later, he reached his destination and jumped off the bus and walked toward the dingy pool hall frequented by Viper and his crew. When he walked in, he was stopped at the door and frisked by a couple of men.

"Where do you think you're going? What's in the bag?" one of them asked.

"Just my school books," Julius replied.

"What are you doing here? Shouldn't you be in the library somewhere, bookworm?"

The other man laughed upon hearing that statement.

"Leave him alone," Viper said as he made his way on crutches over to the men. "I know this kid. You're Denim's friend, right?"

Julius nodded and said, "Yes, I'm Julius."

Viper walked him over to the pool table and asked, "What are you doing here?"

Julius sat down on a stool and said, "I need to talk to you about something."

Viper waved off the two men and picked up a pool stick and said, "Okay, talk."

With sweat forming on his forehead, Julius realized he was trembling as he watched Viper hit the balls into the pocket. He tried to swallow the lump in his throat, but it wouldn't budge, so he forced the words out of his mouth. "I heard some guy took a shot at you the other day."

Without looking up, Viper said, "Somebody's always trying to take a shot at me for some reason or another."

"Do you think it could be revenge over something you did to them?" Julius asked nervously.

Viper stopped playing pool for a second and asked, "What's this about, kid?"

"Who's the guy that shot at you at the barbecue joint?"

He laughed.

"You heard about that, huh?"

"Everybody knows about it," Julius answered. "That was the day you had your accident with Denim."

"Yeah, that's too bad. I'm glad she didn't get hurt too bad. Anyway, that was some fool that's been pissed off ever since his brother was put six feet under because he didn't know how to conduct business. He'd better hope I don't find his non-shooting ass."

"What's his name?" Julius asked as Viper knocked a ball in the corner pocket.

Viper motioned for the bartender to bring him a bottle of beer. "They call him Rock. Why? Do you know him?" he asked.

Julius rubbed his forehead and said, "I had the pleasure of meeting him today, when he pulled a gun on me."

Viper took a sip of beer and frowned. "Why did he pull a gun on you?"

"His little brother threw a snake on Denim at school today, so after school I hunted him down and kicked his ass," Julius revealed, trying to appear tough. "His brother rolled up on us and pulled out a gun."

Viper laid the pool stick down and asked, "Is Denim okay?"

"Yeah, but it scared her pretty bad."

"Why did he throw a snake on her?"

Julius hopped off the bar stool and said, "Because she saved you from a burning car."

Viper grabbed Julius by the arm and asked, "Are you serious?"

"Yeah, I'm serious. Look, Viper, I need to get home, but there's something I have to tell you."

He sat, finished off the beer, and said, "I'm listening."

Julius's heart started pounding in his chest. He was going to do it. He was going to reveal his most feared secret to the man he feared the most, and it made him sick to his stomach.

"I was in the store the night you shot Remy. I saw the whole thing."

Viper dropped his crutches and nearly fell upon hearing that revelation. He stared at Julius and said, "No way."

Julius nodded and said, "No, it's the truth. After you shot him, you walked to the back of the store, grabbed a case of beer, and walked out."

Viper couldn't take his eyes off Julius. Who in their right mind would put their life on the line like this and not expect deadly repercussions?

He picked up his crutches and asked, "Why are you telling me this? Do you have a death wish or something?"

"No, I'm just tired of looking over my shoulder, like you are. That guy, Rock, will eventually catch up with you, and if you get to him first, there will always be another Rock out there, waiting to take a shot at you for something you did to someone they loved. Hell, maybe even someone from Remy's family."

Angry, Viper asked, "What do you want from me, kid? Why are you telling me this?"

"I'm telling you because I don't want to be labeled a snitch or end up dead for what I know. I've been lying to live for weeks, and I'm sick of it. I think you've outgrown this city. It would probably be in your best interest to start over somewhere else."

Viper laughed and asked, "Are you trying to run me out of town, kid?"

"Would you rather be locked up for life or have a needle in your arm?" Julius asked.

Viper pulled out a gun and said, "I could kill you right now and dump your body in the river and no one would ever know."

Lying, Julius said, "Yes, they would, because I made a videotape confession about everything. I put it in a safe place, so if anything happened to me or I came up missing, my parents and the police would know why. I think you should go to jail for what you did, but living around here will make it hard for me to turn you in. I'm giving you an out by suggesting that you leave town. It's best for all of us."

Viper started laughing and tucked the gun back in his waistband and said, "You can forget it, kid, because I'm not going anywhere, and for the record, I didn't mean to shoot the store clerk. That was an accident."

Before Julius could respond, an argument broke out between one of Viper's men and a guy at the pool table next to them. This distraction stopped their conversation and caused the two men at the door to move away from their post. That was when the room erupted in a hail of gunfire, and Julius was struck and fell to the floor.

Chapter Nine

"He's okay," the paramedic said as Julius came to. He was disoriented and had no idea what had happened to him.

"What happened?" Julius whispered.

"You're okay. You just got hit with some broken glass," the paramedic revealed.

"What happened to Viper? The guy I was talking to?" Julius asked.

Detective Daniels leaned down over Julius and said, "He didn't make it, son, but you got us everything we needed to charge him with killing that store clerk."

Julius sat up and asked, "What do you mean? He's dead?"

"It's not the way we wanted this to end. We wanted him alive, but somebody else wanted him dead."

When Julius looked up, he saw Rock, the man who had pulled a gun on him, being put on a stretcher in handcuffs.

"Did that guy shoot Viper?" Julius asked.

Detective Daniels looked across the room. "Yes. Mr. Jackson had a lot of enemies. We've had you under surveillance for some time now in hopes of getting the evidence we needed to get to the truth, but we didn't expect anything like this to go down," the detective confessed.

Angry, Julius said, "You almost got me killed!"

"We're sorry about that, but we protected you as much as possible. You see that gentleman over there?" he asked as he pointed to a large, unshaven man leaning against the pool table. "That's Detective Dunn. He's one of the best undercover officers in our division, and he was able record your conversation with Mr. Jackson before the shooter came in and shot Mr. Jackson. Detective Dunn was watching over you the entire time, so when the shooter came in and shot at Mr. Jackson, he shot the assailant. You were the only witness to the murder at the store, and we weren't getting any cooperation from you, so we had to do what we had to do. It's behind you now. We got the confession we needed, and we got our man."

Julius looked over and saw Viper's body on the floor, covered with a sheet. He couldn't believe how close he had come to dying, but he was glad that it was over.

Detective Daniels helped Julius up and said, "Come on. Let's get you home. You shouldn't have been here, anyway. He could've killed you if we hadn't had you under surveillance."

As Julius stood, he noticed blood on the wall. As he walked out of the pool hall, the glass crunched under his feet. Outside he saw Viper's entourage in handcuffs in the back of a couple of police cars. On the way home all Julius could think about was how angry his father was going to be. He was happy that justice had been served for the store clerk, but he felt a sense of sadness given that he had basically watched a man die . . . until he remembered that it could've been him.

When they arrived at Julius's house, the detective walked him to the door and explained to his parents what had happened and why Julius had the bandage on his head. Mrs. Graham was in tears as she hugged her son, but Mr. Graham immediately yelled at the detective for allowing his son to be put in harm's way. Before slamming the door in the detective's face, Mr. Graham let him know that he planned to sue the police department for their reckless behavior.

Then he hugged his son and told him how much he loved him.

Exhausted, Julius skipped dinner and headed straight to bed. It wasn't until he was safe in the confines of his room that he really exhaled and thought about what he had been through over the past few weeks. He had a major headache, but before going to bed, he called Domingo and told him everything that had happened at the pool hall. Domingo couldn't believe his ears, and while he was thankful his friend was not hurt, he was also angry that he'd gone to the pool hall alone. Before hanging up, Julius asked Domingo to call Denim and tell her what happened so she wouldn't worry that someone would attack her again for her association with Viper. Once Julius ended his call, his little sister, Zakia, entered his room to check on him. She was a brat at times, but he loved her dearly.

She touched his bandage and asked, "Does your head hurt?"

He could see the concern in her eyes, so he smiled and said, "Just a little bit."

Zakia climbed onto the bed with her brother and hugged his waist. "Can I stay in here with you for a while?"

He kissed her forehead and said, "Of course you can."

Zakia started softly singing to her brother, and before long Julius drifted off the sleep, and so did Zakia.

Epilogue

Two months later Julius joined Dré on the basketball court for the opening game. His grades were good, and after some convincing conversations with Dré and Denim, he decided to try out for the team, and he made it. Surprisingly, not only did he make the basketball team, but his skills also allowed him to make the varsity team as a freshman, something not accomplished by many. Julius was no longer being tutored by Denim, but they maintained a close friendship, and he was happy to see her cheering for them on the sidelines. Denim was happy to see the smile back on Julius's face. He had been so unhappy for a long time, and now she knew why.

Before the tip-off of the ball game, Denim blew Dré a kiss and quickly pulled her denim diary out of her purse so she could jot down her thoughts.

As I look at Julius, so happy on the basketball court, I think he's finally found a place to fit in. Life is hard enough on freshmen coming into high school. The burden he was carrying, and the fear he must've felt after witnessing the murder, had to have been eating him alive, and it affected him emotionally and mentally. I hope that I was able to help Julius in some way and that he knows that I'll always be here for him and so will Dré. It's senior year and the last season that I'll get to cheer for my school, but tonight is less about me and more about Julius and his new beginnings. Julius, I love you. Make me proud tonight, and show your teammates, classmates, and the city what you're made of. Somebody has to take Dré's place on the court once he graduates. LOL!

Smooches!

D

The referee blew the whistle for the tip-off, so Denim tucked her diary back into her purse and began cheering, as she had done each year. By the end of the game Dré had scored thirty-two points and Julius had racked up twelve. It was an amazing feat for Julius, and his parents couldn't be prouder. It seemed that things were turning around for the family. His father had found a job that paid more than the previous job he'd had, and they were lucky to find a home in a safer and nicer neighborhood. Their son had blossomed in only a few months, and so had their lives, especially with Julius and his father finding employment. They had no doubt that the best was yet to come.